Landscape with Dog

Landscape with Dog
and Other Stories

by Ersi Sotiropoulos
translated from the Greek by Karen Emmerich

First published in 2010 by

Clockroot Books
An imprint of Interlink Publishing Group, Inc.
46 Crosby Street
Northampton, Massachusetts 01060
www.clockrootbooks.com

Library of Congress Cataloging-in-Publication Data
Soteropoulou, Erse, 1953–
[Short stories. English. Selections]
Landscape with dog and other stories / by Ersi Sotiropoulos ; translated from the
Greek by Karen Emmerich.—1st American ed.
     p. cm.
Translation of selected stories from: O Vasilias tou fliper and Ahtida sto skotadi.
ISBN 978-1-56656-773-2 (pbk.)
1. Greece—Fiction. 2. Short stories, Greek—Translations into English. 3.
Soteropoulou, Erse, 1953—Translations into English. I. Emmerich, Karen. II.
Soteropoulou, Erse, 1953– Vasilias tou phliper. English. III. Soteropoulou, Erse,
1953– Ahtida sto skotadi. English. IV. Title.
PA5630.O825A6 2009
889'.334—dc22
                                                    2009025586

Cover image © Earthshots / Dreamstime.com
Book design by Juliana Spear

We gratefully acknowledge the editors of the publications in which the following
stories appeared: "Can Anybody Hear Me?" in *Words Without Borders*, "Greece:
Inside (and) Out," March 2009. "Rain at the Construction Site" in *Two Lines* 16,
Wherever I Lie Is Your Bed (Fall 2009). "Stella" in *Absinthe: New European Writing*
11 (Spring 2009). "The Woman" in *Metamorphoses* 16.2 (Fall 2008). "Christmas
with Leo" in *or* 3 (October 2009) and "Where Is Piazza Navona?" in *or* 4 (April
2010). "The Pinball King" was featured in the September 2009 issue of the *Brooklyn
Rail.* "An Almost Guinea Fowl" in the *Literary Review* 53.1 (Fall 2009). "Wanna
Play?" was originally commissioned for the New Symposium on Justice, which was
organized by the International Writing Program at the University of Iowa and the
Fulbright Foundation and took place in Paros, Greece, in 2007.

to L.

1992–2009

freehand

There's no such thing as experience. We learn nothing. The body knows nothing. Like a deaf man covering his ears, baffled by inexplicable sounds, like a blind man stretching out a hand in the dark, eyes burning in the briny light of a reflection he suspects is there…

"Each of us is a blind man at a window," I said.

"Shut up and eat," Vera said, laughing.

It was Sunday afternoon and we were having pot roast and potatoes with rosemary. I liked it but wanted something more. The problem with Vera and me has always been one of timing. My wife likes to wake up in the middle of the night and start a conversation. I prefer to talk while we're eating; food enhances my philosophical mood, or perhaps it's the other way around.

"You know what Giacometti said?" I asked, my mouth full.

"The roast seems a little salty to me… what do you think?" she replied.

She got up to clear the table and I did too. I really wanted to tell her this thing about Giacometti because I knew if I left it until later I would forget. I was waiting for the right moment to get her attention and bring it up again.

"So, Giacometti said…" I began.

"Look at that, we're almost out of detergent," she said. Her voice was colorless, with a tinge of disappointment.

Anyone else in my position would have gotten angry, but not me. I knew my wife well enough to be sure her mood was neither ironic nor caustic. Vera liked to think of herself as a practical person, and she always set definite priorities. You could see it even in the way she did the dishes. First she soaped the glasses, then rinsed them with the water running full force, scrubbing insistently at the inside of each with her index finger until she could hear the glass squeak; then she set them on the metal rack to dry. Next she washed the plates, then the silverware, and finally the pots and pans. Vera thinks she's a systematic person, I thought, smiling to myself as she handed me the frying pan. I took a clean towel, dried the pan carefully and put it away. Vera stretched out her arm without looking at me and handed me the roasting pan. "Careful, it's dripping," she murmured. She looked around, still not satisfied. She grabbed the sponge and started to scrub the sink while I wiped the countertops. Then the phone rang.

"Are you going to get it?" Vera asked as she shook her hands dry and ran into the hall.

I looked at the dishes gleaming on the rack. Two plates, two glasses, two forks, two knives: everything in pairs, nothing superfluous. The afternoon sun slanted through the window, giving them a rosy glow, and as I stood there I felt a shiver of tenderness. Then I noticed that the cupboard over the sink was ajar and everything inside was in disarray, open boxes of rice, spilled coffee, empty bottles of olive oil, an old strainer. I'd have to take care of that at some point. Throw out the useless things, tidy up the ones worth keeping. For me, though, order is a form of disorder. Take a face, for instance. Everyone says the face is the mirror of the soul. Is there anything more harmonious than a beautiful face? Yet at the same time, is there anything more terrifying? Anything more monstrous or unnatural? What Giacometti said was right—though I couldn't remember if he'd said it or written it. But did it really matter? Let's just say Giacometti was setting out to draw a face. If he started with the chin, he'd be afraid he might never reach the nose. The longer he sketched and the harder he tried to create a faithful representation, the more it resembled a skull. The only thing left was the gaze. So what he ended up drawing was a skull with a gaze. It made my blood freeze just thinking about it.

"Who was it?" I asked Vera when she came back into the kitchen.

"Wrong number," she said.

That night we went to bed early. Every Sunday there's a detective movie on TV and I like to watch it in bed. "The suspense is terrible," Vera said at some point, wrapping herself around me. I was pleased at the prospect of watching the movie together to the end, something that rarely happened, but soon I felt her breath deepening and her arm growing heavier on my chest. I freed myself gently, then switched off the bedside light and turned down the volume. The movie was over and the credits were scrolling down the screen when it started to rain. The temperature had dropped and my wife pushed her feet toward me, looking for mine. "Want me to warm you up?" I asked. She murmured something, turned to face me and put her arms around me again. I felt for her feet under the comforter and rubbed them between my own. "Better now?" I asked.

Outside the rain was falling more heavily. The TV screen was covered in snow but I couldn't find the remote in the covers. For a while I lay motionless under the comforter, listening to the rain falling hard on the roof like a lullaby. Then I heard a thump and something creaking somewhere in the house and decided to get up. A gust of cold air hit me when I opened the bedroom door. I walked barefoot down the hall. I remembered having closed the window that evening, but now it was open. I tried to shut it but it was caught on something. I felt around in the frame and my fingers brushed up against the round shell of a snail. It was frighteningly smooth under my fingernail. When we first met, Vera was crazy about snails and we ate them all the time. Then one night she pushed her plate away and said in disgust, "Just imagine someone pulling you out of your house and popping you in his mouth!" I'd never thought about it that way, but I had to admit she was right.

I put the snail out on the sill, shut the window and went back down the hall to the bedroom. I slipped under the covers and fell asleep immediately. If I even had time to dream it must have been very brief because soon Vera started to twist and turn and cough. I tried to ignore her and keep sleeping. When I opened my eyes, she was sitting on top of the sheets, propped up with two pillows behind her back.

"Let's say you're facing a firing squad," she said, pulling the comforter toward her side of the bed. "They ask you what your final request is. You have three options: you can smoke a cigarette, eat a fabulous meal, or spend a few minutes with a loved one. What would you choose?"

"The third, I guess."

"I'm not so sure," she said, considering.

"Any normal person would choose the third," I said, annoyed.

"Don't raise your voice."

"I'm not raising my voice."

We were quiet for a while. It was completely silent and I wondered if the rain had stopped.

"The third is the most selfish," Vera said slowly, as if counting the syllables. "It means you're not thinking about the other person, you don't care about the pain you'll be causing, making him see you right before you die."

I pulled her close and hugged her. Under other circumstances we would have made love, but not tonight. We just lay there with her back against my chest. I was so tired my eyes were closing, and I hoped she would fall asleep again soon.

"You're one of those people who think a cow exists just because they looked at it," she said contemptuously.

"What are you talking about?" I murmured.

"The cow exists all on its own, whether you see it or not!"

She drew away from me and got up.

"Come on, let's go to sleep," I pleaded.

I heard her going into the bathroom and turning on the faucet. Then it was quiet. I flipped onto my stomach and put the pillow over my head. In my sleep I heard a sound sweeping toward me in concentric circles, stopping, then starting again. I thought I heard Vera walking past me in bare feet, closing the door behind her, going to the phone and speaking in a whisper.

When I woke up it was morning and a faint light was filtering through the shutters. Vera was lying face up on the bed, staring at the ceiling. We've been together for over five years but I have to admit that even now, each morning I'm surprised to see her. Each morning is a pleasant surprise. Though not exactly beautiful, her face has a kind of pulse, an inner emotion. It's her face, and it's unique. If Giacometti started to draw her chin, I thought, who knows if he would ever get to the nose? He might pause at the corner of her mouth, trying to sketch those thin, petulant lips, then suddenly realize he was drawing a skull again and stop drawing once and for all. A skull with a gaze, what a chilling thought. Fortunately my wife didn't look anything like a skull. Her skin was smooth and tight and covered its bones perfectly. I tried to remember what she had said in the middle of the night about the cow, and what it was that had upset her so much. First Vera had asked me something about a firing squad, then the atmosphere soured and she became hostile. Now everything was confused in my mind. A cow in front of a firing squad? It was complete nonsense. There was no point in fighting over such stupid things.

"Come here," I whispered and reached out to touch her shoulder. Vera drew away to the edge of the bed and turned her back on me. I propped myself up on my pillow so I could see her better.

"Hey, silly," I said. "Even now, if I were in front of the firing squad and they asked me for my final request, I would ask to see you."

Her mouth knotted and her eyes grew big and round, as if she were choking. Then they filled with tears. For a minute it seemed as if she couldn't breathe, but then her breathing returned to normal. "Get away from me," she said calmly. She wiped away her tears and got out of bed. I heard the bathroom door slam, then the water in the shower running full force, pounding against the tiles.

I got up and went over to the window. The rain had washed the sidewalk clean and the grills of the storm drains gleamed in the morning light. The cluster of tenements down the street hung like a bunch of grapes from the sky; in the distance, the slopes of the mountain were still sunk in night. I'd heard once that in winter wolves come down into the city, and right then that image got stuck in my mind. A radiant wave of fear passed through me. From where I was standing the horizon seemed divided in two, half in darkness, half in light.

the pinball king

for P.I.I.

There were four of us in the Fiat, the Italians, my brother
and I. We had set out for Delphi in the early afternoon,
driving that wreck of a car for hours along a rural road
that wove this way and that through the mountains, the
asphalt gaping with potholes. I don't remember what year
it was. It must have been right before Christmas or just
after the holidays, or perhaps one of those anonymous
days of brief lethargy between Christmas and New Year's.
I hadn't eaten since the night before, but I felt full. The
indigestion had stuck in my head like a permanent cramp,
a heaviness brought on by the repeated sight of roast
turkey, mashed potatoes, and kourabiedes.

At regular intervals the headlights would illuminate a
road sign, usually faded or plastered with the photograph
of some local politician, or mutilated and crumpled as if
it had been hit by lightning; the Italians, a couple in their
forties, would make some witty comment and my brother
and I would continue the joke from the back seat. By now
it was evening and outside the car the horizon was gathering in on itself, low and misty, and signals from distant
villages glimmered briefly in the dirty light. At a crossroads, after a moment's hesitation, we took a narrow road
that sloped downhill, winding into a ravine. The only sign
we saw warned of rockslides and showed three black boul-
ders sliding down out of nothing and falling into nowhere.

"Everyone put on their helmets," my brother said, snickering, but the Italians didn't respond.

The road was becoming increasingly steep, with a cliff on one side and on the other thick shrubs that obscured the way ahead. Soon we turned onto a dirt road and soon after that we were lost. Ugo drove for a few more kilometers, bouncing on his seat, leaning into the curves and embracing the wheel with his whole body. Then suddenly he stopped short. We were facing a clearing. The road ended there.

"Scouts, forward march," I ordered, but again the Italians said nothing. My brother looked at me conspiratorially, smiling faintly in the twilight.

For a few minutes no one spoke. The windows had fogged up from our breath and we wiped them off with our scarves and gloves. Outside night was falling fast, enveloping the deserted landscape in black smoke. Ugo switched on the overhead light and started to fumble around in front of him, behind him, under his seat. Then he emptied the plastic bags of fruit and magazines. He was looking for the map. It was badly printed, on cheap, shiny paper, stuck to the back cover of a guidebook we'd bought at a gas station on our way out of town. When he finally found it, he hastily unfolded it and spread it out on the steering wheel. My brother and I leaned over his shoulder to look. Whoever had drawn the map, who rated archaeological sites according to a system involving tiny figures of Hermes, seemed to think Kallanista—a village near Amphissa adorned with four lopsided, angry-looking little gods—was of greater archaeological interest than Delphi, which had only three. Whoever had drawn the map also seemed to think we had passed Delphi a while back and were now headed for Agrinio.

"Could be," Erica said with that ambiguous, slightly absentminded air that female intellectuals often acquire after thirty-five.

"Does this seem to you like the road that leads to Agrinio, Timbuktu, hell, or anywhere at all?" Ugo burst out.

"How about we get out of the car?" I said.

"How about we stay inside?" said my brother.

Years earlier, when we were living together in Florence, my brother figured out just what button to push to make me do things I didn't want to, and even make it seem as if they'd been my idea from the start. Of course we'd had good times, too.

It's spring. I remember him in a white t-shirt. I'm reading Hegel. I see him slipping soundlessly into the room we share. He's calm and fresh, he never sweats, his shoulder blades open and close gently like the wings of a stork. He walks past our beds, two cots pushed against the wall, and stops in front of the table, directly opposite me. Now he's next to the Durst printer. He thinks for a while. The light is full of lilacs. A gleaming blade of sunlight crosses the room from the open window, slicing the table and separating the two of us. Pigeons are cooing in the airshaft, it must be their mating season. A light breeze is blowing. My brother covers the Durst with a sheet of plastic about two meters long. He walks off, hesitates, comes back again. He looks at me sideways in the linen light. I don't look at him, but I know he's watching me. He takes a few steps, stops, then comes back to where I am.

"What's up, aren't we going for coffee?" he asks.

I look at him over the pages of my book. He seems so innocent. His expression says, Aren't you the one who suggested it? I know what's going to happen, and since I don't want it to, I get up and follow him.

We play pinball like maniacs. We're in the deafmutes' bar, as always. It's where we go for coffee, where we arrange to meet friends, where we make up. Every day. Pinball seems to have a soothing effect on us both. At first everyone thought we were twins. "No," I'd say, "we're engaged," and my brother would walk off and wait at a distance, ready for a fight. I knew it pissed him off, but I could never resist the temptation. One Sunday morning when we came in, still half asleep, we saw on the display panel of one of the two pinball machines the number 153,000, and beneath it the words *NEWSPAPER MAN*, and beneath that, in thick black marker, *THE PINBALL KING*. It was the guy who sold newspapers on the corner, a thin redhead who played like crazy on Saturday nights. For a month we struggled valiantly, separately and together, to beat his score. I got as high as 123,000, my brother a bit lower, and together we did terribly. I think that defeat affected us both. Months later, going into the bar, we would head automatically for the other machine. We couldn't bring ourselves to play under that inscription, *THE PINBALL KING*. We never talked about it, either.

It's spring again. I'm working on my thesis, I've fallen behind. Again the stroll around the Durst. Again the glances, the feints, the shuffling back and forth, and then *Froth on the Daydream*, the book he chooses from the bookshelf and pretends to read. I don't look at him, but I know he's watching me.

"So, are we going to the movies?"

"No."

"Don't you want to?"

"No."

"But weren't you saying that today…"

I'm standing calmly on hot coals.

"Are you losing it? Don't you remember what you said this afternoon?"

That was going too far. He realizes this and turns pale, then tries to find an easy way out of the drama that's already beginning. He plays dumb, his usual move. I start hitting him. I don't know how to hit. I spin around unbelievably fast, throwing punches, not caring where they land. I bellow, roar, cry, he tries to immobilize me with his arms but can't. He falls down. He gets up again. I kick. I have a runner's calves. When we were kids we'd fight for hours, me on the bed, him upright and flushed, hands against feet. I kick like a four-legged beast. The rage rises in my throat, floods my brain. Then through my haze I start to see him again, trying to defend himself, adjusting his moves so as not to really hurt me, since we both know he's stronger. He seems surprised, sincerely surprised, his cowlick waving in the air. He must be wondering where I found this terrible strength. His whole expression is one of unease, eyelids fluttering, mouth staring, pink lips parted. But now it's too late, far too late, I can't stop. I keep spinning. And I hit him, hit him. Much later, after an eternity of strangled instants, of coughing, sweat and shortened breath, I see him before me again, I see his astonishment, the stork's wings, the worry, calm down, it's over, that's it, calm down, his childish face, scrawled all over with clumsy question marks. Okay, I tell myself, enough, stop. I lie back on the bed, try to breathe normally, fix my skirt. My hair is on fire and he's still there, shaken, slightly hunched and very innocent. Five minutes later I've pulled myself together, though I'm still quivering a little. I put on my poncho, he gets his jacket, and we go to the movies. Yes, we go to the movies.

What I'm saying is, things weren't always so rosy. Between my brother and me.

It had started to rain. Not a downpour, but a fine, monotonous rain that creaked as it fell and turned the soil into mud.

"Let's look on the bright side," Ugo said.

"You mean in a positive light?" Erica asked, with a hint of irony.

"Let's get out," I said.

No one spoke. You could smell the tension in the car. I pulled on my coat, put up my hood, and got out. It wasn't completely dark yet, and it was less cold than before. Huge shadows glided indistinctly over the slopes of the mountain, creating a puzzle in all the shades of black.

A strong wind blew on the summit; somewhere branches broke with a pitiful meow. But down here everything was still. The creaking of the rain became less perceptible, then stopped altogether.

"Get in," Erica called, "we're turning around."

But a minute later they were all outside, jumping in place to get the blood flowing.

"So what'll it be tonight, a fish place or a meat place?" Ugo asked and started to laugh to himself, covered from head to toe in alpine gear.

He was in a good mood again, and soon Erica burst out laughing too, and my brother and I pinched one another and made faces in the dark.

"What does a Pontic Greek do before he gets into his coffin?" I asked the Italians, and proceeded to tell them the joke. It was the only one I knew, and I didn't know it very well.

That got us into a discussion about the Pontic Greeks, of whose existence the Italians were entirely unaware, about Hellenism, the Asia Minor disaster, the Dardanelles and so on; the Golden Fleece even made an appearance.

"Serves you right," my brother muttered.

He had a point. I hate serious conversations, especially ones with a beginning, a middle, and an end.

We needed to make some decisions. Someone suggested we go back to the main road and keep going until we reached Delphi, someone else said we should just try to find the nearest hotel. For no reason, the tension had started to build again. Erica stared silently at her boots, hands jammed in her pockets, and at some point Ugo started to shout, his face bright red, the white pompom on his hat tracing figure eights in the dark.

"I'm not going to decide for you," Erica said.

Her voice sounded calm and gentle, but beneath the surface you could hear the whetting of knives.

"I know what we can do," I said, with nothing whatsoever in mind.

No one paid any attention. We were about to get back in the car when we heard a noise. From somewhere close by, in the foothills of the mountain or at the edge of the clearing, came the sound of innumerable little bells. I opened my mouth to say something about the Sirens, then closed it again as the jingling grew louder. A weak light trembled in the dark, then vanished, appearing a minute later ten meters ahead of us.

"Good evening," said a shadow, approaching.

It was a goatherd with his flock, about thirty goats. He had a piece of black oilcloth over his head and shoulders and was smiling.

"Kalimera, efharisto," said the Italians. It was the only Greek they knew.

"We're lost," my brother said.

The goatherd told us what we already knew, that we'd taken a wrong turn at the crossroads. He looked very young, but all his teeth were rotten and his back was hunched.

"Where are we now?" I asked.

"Five kilometers outside Kallanista."

I translated for the Italians.

"Kallanista... Kallanista... it was meant to be," they said, remembering the map.

"Are the lady and gentleman foreigners?" the goatherd asked.

He stood up as straight as his hunched back would allow and pronounced the words slowly, with a certain formality.

"Italians," I said.

"One face, one race," the goatherd said and laughed. A gold-capped canine shone in his mouth.

The goats were bounding around by the car, and he lifted his staff and gestured toward them, full of pride.

"Brrr… brrr…" he shouted in mock anger. "Brrr… away from the car." He picked up a rock and pretended to take aim. "They're just playing," he said, turning back to us and letting the rock slip from his hand.

He offered to lead us back to the road to Kallanista, but first we had to stop at his house. Besides, it was right next to the fatal crossroads.

"Otherwise my wife will be angry," he said.

I translated for the Italians. The goatherd stood waiting before us, watching keenly as we spoke.

"Why will she be angry?" Erica asked.

"What did the lady say?" the goatherd asked, his eyes burning with impatience.

"She's worried we'll be late," my brother said.

"My wife will kill me," the goatherd said, looking Erica in the eye.

I translated again, and without any more fuss we got in the car and set off. And so for two or three kilometers we paraded through the night, the goatherd out front with his prancing herd, us following behind, taking care not to hit any stray goats. Every so often one of them would run off toward the mountain and he would chase after it, and when he caught it would nod reassuringly in our direction. Now and then he would turn and wave to us with his staff, his face small and dark under the black oilcloth that covered his whole body, though it had stopped raining a while ago.

"Deus ex machina," said Ugo, rolling his window down for the fourth time and sticking a hand out to answer the goatherd's wave.

"Nuisance ex machina," Erica muttered, but fortunately they didn't start fighting.

The goatherd's house was built into the foot of the mountain, ten meters back from the dirt road. We entered a large, low-ceilinged room strewn with sheepskins and braided rugs. Coals were burning in a bronze brazier in a corner under a wooden iconostasis bearing tiny icons of saints. The space was warm and heavy with smells. There was a sweetish sense of enclosure and somewhere inside the house steam rose from a dish boiling on a propane burner.

"Sit down, sit down," said the goatherd's wife, coming over to us.

She was a plump girl, short, dressed in black, with a bright red face that looked as if it had caught fire. She seemed to be expecting us.

"Offer them something, woman," the goatherd said and went back out to put his goats in the fold.

Sitting by the brazier, we drank cognac and ate olives and feta. We were all very pleased with the turn our adventure had taken. My brother took off his shoes and wiggled his toes in his socks, and soon the rest of us did the same.

"Brrr… brrr…" Erica said, looking at Ugo.

"Brrr…" he answered, laughing.

"I heard you two hours ago, passing in your car," the woman said, and I translated.

She didn't sit down, but stood beside us, watching and waiting. Ugo lit his pipe and she ran right away to get an ashtray.

"You think she'd sell that thing?" Ugo said, looking at the iconostasis. He blew the smoke away from his face and for an instant the figure of St. George disappeared, so that all you could see was the dragon with its toothy green tail.

"Shame on you," Erica said, but her tone sounded encouraging to me.

My brother and I exchanged glances, and when he didn't say anything, I explained to the Italians how it was impossible, because if we asked them for anything, they'd feel obliged to give it to us for free, and so on and so forth.

"Here comes our deus ex machina," Erica said, putting an end to the conversation.

The goatherd came into the room, tossed off the oilcloth and walked over to us.

"You let these people go hungry, woman?" he said loudly and, without waiting for a reply, sat down beside us.

He filled our glasses with cognac and made a toast to the Italians, saying that Italy was a beautiful country, like Greece, and that the Italians had been our friends during the war. "Buenasera, senorita," he said to Erica and drained his glass.

In the light his face seemed even younger, almost childlike, with a long scar that ran from his left eyebrow to his ear. When he saw me looking at it, he said he'd been bitten by a mule when he was twelve, then told a story about a band of animal thieves who had been wreaking havoc on that part of the country back then. As he spoke, he slowly stroked his cheek with his thumb, as if to make sure his scar was still there.

We ate for two hours straight—bean soup, smoked herring, potatoes, raw onions from the garden, eggs from their hens, then all over again from the beginning. The wife would bring out a platter and go right back into the kitchen to prepare something else; the only time she spoke was to tell her husband to change his shoes, which were caked in dried mud.

"In the morning we'll slaughter a pig," the goatherd said, and raised his glass to clink it against ours. "Eviva... To our health."

"To our health," we all said. "Salute, salute."

He poured us another round.

"Salute," Ugo said and glanced at his watch.

"Why are you in such a rush?" the goatherd asked him.

"It's late and he has to drive," my brother answered without bothering to translate.

The goatherd looked at us as if he couldn't believe his ears.

"In the morning we'll slaughter a pig," he said emphatically.

One night in Florence as I was coming home, I saw a rat in the front entrance, staring at me, paralyzed with fear. It seemed lost, standing petrified under the arch of the stairwell, sniffing uneasily. Its glassy eyes blinked when I turned on the light and in the fraction of a second that we looked at each other, its expression reminded me of something that I couldn't quite place. For a long time, that encounter left a certain aftertaste, not of disgust or fear, but like an event suspended between fantasy and reality, something familiar yet indefinable, like when you hear an echo of voices when there's no one else in the room, or when you think you recognize a silhouette on the street and follow it for a few blocks, then turn down some other street without finding out who it was.

"In the morning we'll slaughter a pig," the goatherd repeated. "Translate that," he said, turning to me as if I were responsible for how the night would unfold.

I tried to explain the situation to the Italians. We were all a little drunk, and drugged by the bean soup and smoked herring. My brother was talking about some old roommate of his who'd been a champion burper and Ugo said something about Guiseppe di Salvo, a count and specialist in heraldry who also happened to be a champion farter, and they both kept at it, adding spice to their stories, the four of us laughing until tears came to our eyes, as across from us the goatherd read our lips, trying to understand.

When I told my brother about the rat, he said he didn't care, it didn't matter what the rat reminded me of, what mattered was that we were shelling out a pile of money to live in a dump.

"We have to tell the signora," he concluded, then stood and walked out of the room.

"What does the one thing have to do with the other?" I called to his back.

"A lot," he answered from the kitchen.

I heard him open the oven, pull out a pan and stir the dish with a metal spoon—it was giant beans in tomato sauce, I think.

"Because," he continued, coming back in, "pretty soon you'll start wondering what the rat thinks of you, and before you know it you'll end up like that girl on the boat."

The previous summer he had gone on a week-long sailing trip. One night when the waters were rough they had to anchor unexpectedly a half mile off an uninhabited island, Oxia, because the boat was in danger of smashing against the rocks. The boat belonged to a friend of my brother's; there was another friend with them, and a girl from Athens. As soon as it got dark, she started ranting about the souls of people who die violent deaths at sea and return at night to the surface of the water to talk to the living. She looked panicked and at some point started babbling incoherently, saying that the ghost of some diver who had disappeared in those waters and whose body had never been found was going to come after her to settle the score.

"What does that lunatic have to do with what I just told you? What does the one thing have to do with the other?" I asked. The rage was gathering inside me, pressing against my temples.

"What other? Why do you always need there to be something else?" my brother said and left the room.

I heard the front door slam behind him and his footsteps as he ran down the stairs.

"Now you know what the Dionysian spirit is," Ugo said.

We were back in the Fiat, headed toward Kallanista. We'd left the goatherd and his wife standing in front of their house, waving and smiling, though looking a little baffled, as if they couldn't believe we weren't going to stay there that night and celebrate the slaughtering of the pig with them in the morning. During the whole of our long, drawn-out departure, as we stood in the cold exchanging wishes and thanks with the columns of our breath rising tremulously into the dark sky, only the occasional bleating of an insomniac goat disturbed the frozen solitude of the landscape. At last, when they were finally convinced that we were determined to go, the goatherd's wife presented Erica with a big chunk of feta wrapped in cheesecloth and we set off.

"Why bring the Dionysian spirit into it, when all you really want to say is that they're good people?" Erica said a while later.

"An endangered species," my brother said.

"Simple, good people," Erica stressed.

"And we're pigs," I said, and nervous laughter seized us all.

I had leaned my head on my brother's shoulder and for a few minutes I pictured the pig snoring blissfully in its sty, unaware that the crucial moment was approaching.

"People often posit an opposition between the Dionysian and Apollonian spirits. But they're wrong, totally wrong," Ugo began again. "They present them as if they were two opposite poles. But that's clearly a misunderstanding on the part of Western philosophers, particularly the Germans. Western thought is incapable of comprehending that Eastern quality. I mean, a more holistic approach…"

He was talking mostly to keep himself awake.

"This feta is dripping on my feet," Erica muttered.

No one spoke after that and we continued on our way in a torpid silence.

We're sitting on the balcony of the hotel in Kallanista, looking out into the night. I came outside to smoke and then my brother followed. The Italians said goodnight and went to their room. The two rooms share a balcony, so we don't turn on the light, in case we might wake them up. It's cold. We're sitting side by side in the dark, staring out at the thick black screen in the distance, on which the scattered lights from the village mingle with the pale stars. I think again of the incident with the rat, then about other moments from our life together in Florence. There are lots of things I'd like to ask my brother and I try to put my thoughts in some kind of order. Episodes from our childhood crowd untidily in my mind as we stare silently into the frozen night, not speaking because we have nothing to say, while from the other room come the first indistinct sounds of the Italians making love.

"Brrr..." my brother whispers, but I can't laugh. "Brrr..." he repeats half-heartedly.

A rat is just a rat, I tell myself. Siblings will always be siblings. I breathe deeply and the cold air sticks in my throat like salt. I swallow, but the saliva won't go down. I think about how there's nothing to think about, no rat, just flashbacks of old photographs, scenes from birthdays, amusement parks, summer vacations. We're two kids in a happy family, school's out, we're piling our furniture into the back of a truck and heading to the country, there's no room for drama, I tell myself. We're two adorable little kids in white socks eating fried eggs over spinach rice, with a seven-thirty bedtime and a live-in maid. That was the most anyone could dream of in the devastated Greece of the '60s. My brother would wake up during the night and scream. If I cover my ears, I can still hear those frantic cries, can smell the panic moving from room to room like an electric discharge. The lights come on, the maid runs down the stairs, his body clenches and coils in his bed as he's seized with spasms, his face distorted by pain. There's no reason for these attacks. No reason? We're allies in agony, I think, and glance at him. His profile seems stubborn, uneasy, like a crooked sketch about to be swallowed up by the darkness. We're enemies in agony. That's what the look in the rat's eyes reminded me of. Enemies,

enemies. What agony? There's no agony. Don't go digging up tragedies. The bottom of my mind is a smudged sheet of paper; the words get erased before I have a chance to read them.

Through the balcony door come Erica's weak sighs.

"Bella, bella... come sei bella..." Ugo grunts.

Then there's silence for a few minutes.

Now they're talking, but too quietly for anyone to hear. Someone is crying. Crying or trying to come. Silence. Footsteps. They push the bed against the wall. Again we hear Erica's sighs, at first like breathing, secret and congested, then louder and louder, with a screechy undertone.

"Bella, bella..." Ugo roars.

Then there's a thump.

"Bella, you'll fall," my brother whispers, and our eyes meet.

For an instant I feel like he's looking away, but I'm wrong because he keeps staring at me, then suddenly sticks out his tongue and we start to laugh. I hug him, he pulls me by the elbow and we go back inside.

We left for Delphi early the next morning. It was sunny. The windows were covered with fingerprints, and a wheezing winter sun slipped into the car and nipped at our skin through our sweaters. It was terribly hot, but the Italians didn't want to open a window.

"Are you crazy? There'll be a draft, we'll catch cold," Ugo protested, repeating his familiar theory that it's better to be naked in Antarctica than to get caught in a draft in warm weather.

My brother and I looked at each other. In the stony white light his eyes were almost transparent, smashed irises under papery lids. The heat became more and more suffocating as we drove. Outside Delphi the goatherd's package of feta began to stink and we threw it away in a parking lot on the side of the road.

an almost guinea fowl

for Kay

Telis came home that afternoon in high spirits. The crisp air had relieved his headache. The atmosphere in the small apartment was pleasant, if a bit stuffy. Everything was orderly and peaceful. It was perfectly quiet, Maro must have taken the baby for a walk. He opened the balcony door and stepped outside to admire his plants. He had arranged the pots in the best way possible on the narrow balcony. Of course it was a northern exposure, and the adjacent buildings cut down on the light, and since the apartment was on the fourth floor the wind was often strong. But thanks to his calculations, before long they would have a little jungle out there.

He leaned over the railing and looked down. The traffic on the avenue was dense and chaotic. He went back inside and closed the door. It was April now, and though the days had grown perceptibly longer and the trees along the street were bright green, with heavy, lustrous leaves, this week had brought a sudden stretch of bad weather. As he walked past the mirror in the hall he smiled. The cold spell allowed him to wear a sweater under his jacket, which made his tie sit better. For a young lawyer these things mattered.

He went into the kitchen to get a beer.

Babe, I bought you a very special guinea fowl. I won't be late. I LOVE YOU, read the note on the table.

They had gotten into the habit of leaving one another notes in the early days of their relationship, or rather after they had silently agreed that things were getting serious. Maro had started calling him "babe" after the baby was born. At first it amused him, but then it started to get annoying. "But don't you see, it's because the baby hasn't changed *anything* between us," she would say.

"A very special guinea fowl," he said to himself as he opened the fridge. That meant it had cost more than they could afford.

He was drinking a beer in front of the open fridge door when the idea took shape. The telephone rang. Without hurrying, he went into the hall, the can in his hand.

"Christos, I was just thinking about you," he said. "I was about to call."

"..."

"Maro bought a guinea fowl, she got it from a hunter."

"..."

"Free range, it's been doing somersaults in the hills and dells."

"..."

"You two should come for dinner. We can watch the match, too."

He winked at Maro, who had just gotten home and was pushing the door open with the stroller.

"Great, around eight thirty," he said and replaced the receiver. "Christos and Jeanette are coming for dinner," he said, unbuckling the baby.

"He's fussy today," she said a while later.

They were getting the baby ready for his afternoon nap. He lay him down in the crib while she put the powders and creams back in the cupboard with the diapers. He often thought that this was their best moment as a family. The two of them with the baby. A parenthesis of peace and autonomy.

"There's something I should tell you," Maro began, hesitating. "It's not a guinea fowl."

Telis looked at her incredulously. "You're joking."

"I'm serious, it's not a guinea fowl."

Her expression said that offense was the best defense.

"What kind of game are you playing?" he asked, his voice rising a notch.

He went back into the kitchen. He opened the fridge and took out the bird. Its skin was yellowish and pimply. He kneaded it with both hands, then sniffed it.

"It's a chicken, a plain old chicken," he heard her say behind him.

"Why did you tell me it was a guinea fowl?" he asked, trying to keep calm.

"To make you happy, like that time with the frog's legs."

"What do you mean?"

"I just cut the wings in half. I dipped them in batter and fried them."

Telis was silent for a minute. Maro looked at him and he thought he saw the shadow of a small triumph in her eyes.

"You'd better find a guinea fowl by this evening."

He grabbed her wrist and twisted until the skin was red, the knuckles white.

"Let me go!"

"This is the first time we're having them over since the baby was born."

Telis walked the baby around the apartment until six. Finally, around six-thirty, he managed to put him down. He opened a beer, made a sandwich, and sat down in front of the television. At seven Maro came back weighed down with grocery bags and went straight into the kitchen. Telis drained his beer and followed her in. Four birds lay in a row on the table.

"Duck, goose, turkey, pheasant... I couldn't find a guinea fowl," Maro said, on the verge of tears.

They all look more or less alike, Telis thought. Only the turkey still had its head. A plucked skull with glassy little eyes.

"There's this, too," Maro said, pointing to a shrink-wrapped package. "Rabbit, already butchered. I paid with the money from the store," she added, as if answering a question. For a few years she had been part owner of a small bookstore. After the baby was born she'd sold her share.

"Which should we choose?" Telis wondered.

He put an arm around her shoulders and they bent together over the table.

"Which should we choose?"

"They look so defenseless," Maro said after a while, drawing her index finger along the turkey's back. As she leaned over the table to look at the birds her ass showed round and tight under the thin fabric.

"Shhh…" Telis whispered. "They're vultures… come on, follow me…"

He took her hand and led her into the bedroom. He pulled down her panties and entered her from behind, gently and almost indifferently, as if he had something else on his mind. Then he gave a few hard thrusts, waiting to hear her breathing grow short, to deepen and change. He pulled out, then started to move in and out quickly and rhythmically, maintaining the greatest possible distance between them, so that the tip of his prick sank into her for a fraction of a second before slipping back out again.

"The baby's birth changed him a lot," Maro said as she made a salad.

"That's how it goes," Jeanette replied, blowing smoke.

They were sitting in the kitchen, to keep an eye on the guinea fowl roasting in the oven. The whistles and shouts from the match mingled with the noise of the exhaust fan over the stove.

"He's become very possessive. I have no time to myself anymore."

"The problem with men," Jeanette said, "is that they can't tell their ego from their superego."

Maro set her knife down in the strainer with the lettuce leaves.

"And you know what happens if you have a superego as big as an Olympic stadium and an ego as small as a punching bag…"

She filled her glass with wine and drank it down.

"I have the feeling I'm going to start smoking again," Maro said, reaching for Jeanette's cigarettes.

"We lost by three points," Telis said.

He was clearing all the books and things off the desk so they could set the table. Maro stood there waiting for him, holding the plates and silverware.

"Who wants wine and who wants beer?" Jeanette asked.

"You've had enough already," Christos said.

"Could you cut the bread, please?" Maro asked.

"How about I bring in the wild bird?" Jeanette giggled, then did a pirouette and ran into the kitchen.

"I don't believe it," Christos said.

"Come on, let the women have their fun," said Telis.

The desk was clear and he spread the checked tablecloth, smoothing the creases with his palm.

"The baby's crying," said Maro. "Can you take the plates?"

"A guinea goose with gooseberries," Jeanette said and stood up from the table.

"They were prunes," Maro said.

"I was joking," Jeanette sighed, sinking into the couch. "Who's going to pour me some wine?"

"Wonderful, delicious, pure ambrosia," Christos said, stretching in his chair.

"You ate it all, you cannibals," Telis laughed. "What are you doing, smoking?"

"Just for tonight," Maro said.

"I want wine," Jeanette said again.

The two men carried the dirty plates into the kitchen. Maro took the bottle of wine and sat next to Jeanette on the couch.

"Something's happening to me. I have a little ball with feathers in my stomach," Jeanette murmured.

"You want me to help you to the bathroom?" Maro asked.

"No, pour me some wine."

They sat there silently for a while, their heads resting on the back of the couch.

It must have been after midnight. The hum of the avenue had died down, the building was quiet. Every once in a while they would hear the elevator wheezing as it headed for other floors. The heat had gone off hours ago and the apartment was starting to get cold.

"I only like cooking for friends, like the two of you," Maro said. "Otherwise it's such a bore."

She glanced over to see if Telis was listening.

"I only like cooking for Christos," Jeanette interjected with a little laugh, her tone tender and ironic.

Christos coughed to clear his throat.

"My father and I used to go hunting sometimes. When he was alive, I mean."

He had sat back down in the chair. His elbows were resting on the table and he was looking down at them, his head in his hands.

"We would shoot woodcocks, wild ducks, occasionally a rabbit. I don't remember any guinea fowls."

"You know how I feel?" Jeanette said excitedly. "Like that time we smoked pot on vacation on Santorini."

"I think the baby's crying again," Telis said, looking at Maro.

"Do you want us to leave?" Jeanette asked, half rising from the couch.

"It's still early, we haven't had dessert," Telis said.

"My father was a great hunter," Christos said, as if he were talking to himself. "And a fisherman, too. In the summer he would set trotlines and—"

"Your father was a jerk," Jeanette interrupted, throwing a leg over the arm of the couch.

"The baby's crying, don't you hear?" Telis asked.

Maro lit another cigarette from Jeanette's pack and blew the smoke between her fingers.

"I think it's your turn," she said, her voice flat.

"What did my father ever do to you?" Christos asked.

"He made you really boring," Jeanette replied. Then her voice grew more animated. "Guys, I feel like I'm high."

"You're drunk, that's all," said Christos.

"What are we celebrating today?" Jeanette asked Maro.

"What are we celebrating?" Telis repeated, coming into the living room. "My lovely little wife wanted to cook me something exotic and…"

He looked at Maro, waiting for her to finish his sentence.

"Why don't we play a game?" she suggested.

"Cards," said Christos.

"Biriba," said Telis.

"Truth or dare," said Jeanette.

"Truth or dare," echoed Maro.

"Dare?" Jeanette said, pleased. "Okay, take off your pants and your underwear—that is, if you're wearing underwear," she said, laughing, "and walk around the table three times saying—"

"Forget it," Telis cut her off.

"Come on," Maro egged him on.

Telis licked his lips and looked at each of them in turn. Then he started to unbutton his pants.

"Say 'I was a good boy today, ma'am,' and run around the table."

"Happy?" Telis asked.

He was down to his underwear and socks.

"Are you kidding?" Jeanette said.

"Then I'll take truth," Telis said reluctantly.

"Guys, should we accept?"

"That's cheating!" Maro shouted.

"Just this once, it's fine," Christos said.

"But you have to stay in your underwear," Jeanette said, "and tell me quickly, the truth, have you ever cheated on Maro?"

"Never."

"The truth!"

"Never… while we were married."

"Who was she?" Maro asked.

"He only has to answer one question," Christos said.

"Who was she? Tell me who she was."

"I feel that little ball in my stomach again, it's like it has feathers… or corners, sharp ones…"

"If it has corners, it's not a ball."

"You don't understand."

"I'm dead tired. Let's go."

But he didn't get up.

They were alone in the living room. Telis and Maro had gone into the baby's room.

"I'm sure it's a ball. Do you think I have cancer?"

"Tell me, do you know anything about Telis?"

"Yes."

"Well?"

"What, are you stupid?"

"I want you to tell me who she was," Maro repeated.

She was leaning over the baby's crib, changing his diaper.

"They'll hear us," Telis whispered.

His cheeks were burning. The room was lit only by a nightlight and he hoped she couldn't see his expression.

"If you don't tell me, I'll tell them it wasn't a guinea fowl."

Telis laughed nervously. He was still in his underwear and felt ridiculous.

"Tell them," he said listlessly. "Tell them, if it'll make you feel better."

Maro started to cry, little sobs that kept getting louder. Her tears fell on the baby, who woke up and wriggled around in the crib. She picked him up and pressed his forehead to her wet cheeks. He was warm and very soft, almost spineless, and every so often his little body would give an irritated jerk as if shot through by an electric current. Suddenly he let out a loud shriek and hit her face hard with his head.

"I'm going back," Telis said.

She stood there in the half darkness, with her back against the door and the baby in her arms. They were both crying, pressed up against each other, and the sound of their breathing, fitful and erratic, pierced the milky light of the room.

Christos and Jeanette were holding hands on the couch. They had brought the dessert in from the kitchen, eaten, and left their dirty plates on the floor.

"Come and see my plants," Telis said as he entered the living room.

He'd put on a new pair of pants and was buckling his belt as he walked toward the balcony door. He wasn't sure whether they'd heard the fight and the plants seemed like the best distraction.

"I couldn't possibly move," Christos said.

Jeanette stood up and Christos lay down on the couch.

Out on the balcony it was biting cold. Telis stepped aside to make room for Jeanette.

"This summer we'll have gardenias," he said, bending over a flowerpot where a little shoot was peeking out.

Jeanette looked up at the leaden sky and stretched, about to take a deep breath. But she stopped midway and he heard her exhale impatiently.

"Are you going to tell her?" she asked.

"Are you crazy?"

He turned toward her jerkily and stumbled. They were so close that the scent of her body lotion hit the roof of his mouth and he felt as if he were swallowing wheat and honey.

"Do you want me to tell her?" she asked, squinting her eyes as if searching for some distant star.

Her voice was colorless and strained.

Telis took a quick look into the apartment. Christos was sleeping on the couch, his mouth hanging open. The apartment was a mess. Someone had knocked over the stroller in the middle of the hall.

"Come on, be serious," he said and grabbed her hand.

In the few centimeters that separated them, he felt that her body was a familiar yet threatening thing, and if he came any closer, if he touched her body with his, he would collapse altogether.

"Come on," he said again, "you'll get cold," and pushed her gently inside.

The next morning the sky had cleared and it was still cold. Telis got up early, feeling as if he hadn't slept at all. He had fallen asleep on the couch without a blanket and had shooting pains in his back. The ashtrays were full, the wine had gone sour in the glasses and stank. A war zone, he thought, looking around. For some reason, instead of depressing him, the previous night had lifted his spirits. He began to clean, mentally dividing the apartment into three zones: kitchen, hall, living room. Hope, desire, disappointment. He started with the living room and worked his way in. Hope, desire. He washed the dishes, dried them with a clean cloth and put them away. He felt that the previous night had taught him something and, as he methodically cleaned, he tried to figure out what it was. The message was there inside him, but it kept slipping away. Fragments of thoughts sat in his mind without moving through it, without leaving traces. But his mood remained light, natural, pervading his movements, as he brought order to the chaos around him.

At around seven-thirty the hot water started to come up through the pipes, passing into the radiators with restrained momentum and a hollow purring noise. Telis paced as he drank his coffee. Should he be feeling guilty about this little inspection? The house was now neat and sparkling clean, just as he had found it the previous afternoon.

The baby gurgled in his crib.

Babe, he wrote, *it wasn't anything serious, I love you.* He hugged the baby to him and kept writing. *A near-betrayal,*

feather in the hair

In Piazza Ungheria the waiter was different, no one recognized me. I asked for a cappuccino and a croissant. I was sitting at an outside table, and saw behind my back the long rows of trees with their heavy foliage, the shady sidewalks of Viale Liegi, Viale Regina Margherita meeting Via Nomentana and vanishing in the distance, and beyond that people gathering around a stone fountain where a goldfish thrashed around, out of the water. I didn't turn to look. My limbs were numb and I stretched my legs out in the weak sun. I could feel that same morning coolness, that chill in the air that will develop later into unbearable heat. The waiter brought out my order on a tray and leaned over me politely to be paid. People came and went. I waited in vain for someone I knew to pass by.

Fortunately Carolina was with me. She drained her glass—a cola, I think—and we stood up. We started down Viale dei Parioli, but as we were walking I changed my mind and we turned around. At the corner of Bruno Buozzi and Bertoloni I realized we were lost. We started asking for directions. The answers were contradictory. Depressing ochre buildings, liveried doormen, elderly gentlemen with camelhair overcoats and silver walking sticks, two foreign workers eating lunch beside a parked limousine. Piazza Santiago del Chile. Piazza Don Minzoni. Finally we found Via Monti Parioli and started to ascend. No impatience, not a shred of emotion.

I walked in front, Carolina followed. I headed straight to my old hairdresser Gaetano's salon. I found him standing behind a man with curly hair. "I'll be done in five minutes," he said, waving the blow dryer. The man in the chair looked indifferently at us in the mirror, then became absorbed again in his own reflection, the corners of his mouth crinkling in secret satisfaction. We sat and waited, flipping through magazines. Gaetano's young assistant, wearing lots of makeup and a pink knit jacket, kept walking back and forth and closing the door of the salon, muttering, "There's a draft." But by now the heat was settling in. A young man slathered in oil was baking in front of a tanning lamp in the back room. Gaetano finished and we went to the bar next door for an espresso. You couldn't smoke in the bar so we went outside for a cigarette. "Che bella!" he said about Carolina, whom he remembered from when she was still in my belly. We briefly reminisced about an evening years ago when he came to cook at my house and brought an extraordinary wine from Naples, Greco di Tufo, and we made prank calls all night. A few of my girlfriends had been there, too, and he asked after them. "Now there's caller ID," I said. "No more prank calls," he said.

We kissed and parted. At the flower stall at the top of Via Gramsci Carolina and I stopped and bought a small camellia. Then we descended the hill arguing about something I can't recall. Arnaldo, the porter, was strolling back and forth on the sidewalk in front of the building. "Oh, signora..." he whispered through his fat lips. He pushed open the heavy gate and we went into the courtyard.

Once, during one of her visits, my mother had found the gate closed and didn't feel like ringing the bell, so she scrambled over the fence. "The signora mother is a rock climber!" the porter's wife had said admiringly. That "signora mother" had sounded like a title, as if she were saying the queen mother.

I ran down the stairs. "Signora Tonina," I cried, falling into her arms. She pulled back and gave me an air kiss, her skin cold and slightly sweaty. She had never liked kisses. "I lost an eye," she said, "the left one, to cancer." "You can't tell at all," I said. We sat down. Everything in the basement apartment was neat and clean, the cat's bowls lined up in front of the sink, the light over the table on even though it was day. "D'Amore died," Tonina said. "Just recently he married the Ukranian woman who was taking care of him, she inherited everything and now his daughters are running to the courts." I lit a cigarette, pulled the ashtray closer, and offered her one. "I quit, but I'll take one," she said. The atmosphere in the low-ceilinged room was tepid, a tepid chill combined with the vague but penetrating smell of mildewing walls. "The marquis on the fourth floor went mad, he's got more money than he can count but won't let anyone in to clean, it's a pigsty in there, and he says he's on bin Laden's side, bin Laden's the only one worth anything…"

I looked at Carolina. She was sitting up straight in her chair, listening to the gossip about the building with an enigmatic smile. "What a beautiful girl," Tonina said, then started as if she'd just remembered something. "Sandro," she called. "Sandro, come and say hello." Their son appeared, unexpectedly tall, almost handsome. "He's always busy with his computers, I don't know what to do with him," his mother complained. "He's at the university now, economics." "Business school," Sandro clarified. He pulled up a chair and sat down beside her. We were back where we used to be, sitting in the same configuration as in the old days, the three of them at one end and me across the table, only this time there was Carolina, too. Tonina cleared her throat and leaned toward me confidingly. "You know that almost everyone here went to jail during the Clean Hands campaign." "The whole neighborhood emptied out, Parioli was deserted," Arnaldo said, shaking his head. The way he said it was ambiguous, you couldn't tell if it made him happy or sad. He had spent his life serving marquises and contessas, but even now that they were mixed up in the biggest scandal Italy had seen in recent years, he wouldn't speak openly. His reserve made me think again of something that always made an impression on me: the Italians' respect for hierarchy, regardless of their ideology. During all the years I had lived in this building, I thought the porter and his wife were right-wing, perhaps even fascists; only toward the end of my stay did they tell me they were communists.

They asked us to stay for lunch. I lied and said we were expected elsewhere. They insisted. I refused. We rose. "Why didn't you want to stay? They were really nice," Carolina asked as we left. "I thought you didn't want to," I lied again. The three of them followed us into the courtyard. "Sandro will give you a ride." "There's no need." We went into the garage. We embraced. I gave her an air kiss, too. The car glided toward Piazza delle Belle Arti. I watched absentmindedly as Rome passed by the window, sitting beside the same Sandro I had written about in a short story fifteen years earlier, when he was just a kid, and kind of a brat. We passed by Alberto Moravia's house, those stairs I had once climbed with trembling knees. Sandro dropped us off near Piazza Navona. We ate in a trattoria somewhere in the ghetto, a fried artichoke like a shriveled blackbird.

The visit to the Vatican had none of the drama I had feared, and perhaps inwardly wished for. To make it interesting for Carolina I'd decided to combine it with a tour of the museums and the Sistine Chapel. My plan failed: we woke up at the crack of dawn and stood in line for hours to listen to a cicerone repeating the same short sentences in five different languages. It was past noon when we split off from the group. We walked past St. Peter's and followed the perimeter of the walls. The sun beat down on exhausted tourists who dragged themselves along the sidewalks, wet handkerchiefs pressed to their foreheads. We reached the light at Aurelia and crossed. From a distance I looked for the bar on Via di Santa Maria delle Grazie alle Fornaci, which years ago had been the only one that stayed open all night, a favorite haunt of cab drivers and tramps, where I'd spent many evenings in the half-light, trying to write a line, trying to fit two mutilated words together on a napkin and ignore what was happening to me—what I would later call bottomless unhappiness. The bar wasn't there anymore, a pet supply store had opened in its place. But on the next corner the bar and gaming parlor where I used to play pinball was still there. One day I'd gotten the top score; the owner had been watching me silently, washing glasses behind the counter, and afterward I bought a round for the house. I thought we could stop in for a coffee, but I didn't recognize the guy behind the bar so we kept going. From there on all the streets were named after cardinals: Via Cardinal Agliardi, Via Cardinal Lualdi, and so on.

The little apartment building on the corner with the green railing was just as I had left it. I stopped in the entrance, looked at the names on the buzzers, took a few steps toward the elevator and then turned around. "What are we doing here?" Carolina asked. I went back out to the street and looked at the façade. Which floor was it? The third? Fourth? It must have been the third floor, the cab driver with the blond wife and the twins lived on the fourth, they used to make love in the afternoon, the wooden headboard would hit the wall and make the whole building shake. "I'm bored," Carolina said. I crossed the street and stood on the opposite sidewalk under the burning sun. I looked at the windows on the third floor. The shutters of the one on the corner were tightly closed; there was a desiccated flowerpot and some trash on the sill. I used to leave it open at night. It was fall. I had no table, I put the typewriter on the only chair and knelt in front of it. I would keep rewriting the same page for two months, adding an adjective, changing a verb, writing it all over again from the beginning. The humidity from the Tiber slipped through the window at night; at dawn the bells of St. Peter's stunned me like slaps.

White nights at the Vatican. "I can't take any more," said Carolina.

All that was left was the visit to the embassy. It was our last day. We passed through Villa Borghese on foot. From the entrance to the zoo I could see the falsely cheerful, two-story cake with its small garden. Often at night the chimps' screams disturbed the ambassadors' sweet sleep. The porter wasn't at his post; he'd been replaced by a camera with a red eye. The same slow elevator with the wooden door brought us to the second floor. The circular hallway, the central room with the glass panes, the Piranesi engravings. The parquet creaked in the same spots. Where my desk used to be were the embassy archives. A near-sighted woman looked at me without seeing from behind a pile of folders, then lowered her head again. On our way out, I passed by the ambassador's bathroom. I had never used it before, and noticed that it was much smaller than the employees' bathroom. A half-finished roll of toilet paper sat on top of the yellowing radiator. I flushed, went out and took Carolina's arm; she was impatient to leave.

Fiumicino

Flight AZ 720

Why did you bring me to Rome? Carolina asked.

Why did you want me to come with you?

I didn't answer, I didn't have anything to say. I saw something in her hair, a white piece of fuzz as light as a feather, and reached out a hand to pick it off.

the exterminator

Two German women were sitting at a table by the display case in the pastry shop. They had just ordered. Behind them, beneath the shop's only fan, stood a young woman with a pale face and anxious expression.

She had come to the island at the beginning of the summer to write a book. She'd rented a small house on the hill and shut herself up for a month without speaking to anyone. When she finally decided to go out, the first thing she did was buy three different kinds of tiropitas. She tasted a corner of each, then threw them all out. Biting into the tiropitas she had felt unexpectedly guilty. If she wanted to finish by fall, she would have to concentrate only on writing. So she withdrew into the house again and devoted herself to her work.

"What would you like?" asked the waiter.

"What would I like..." the young woman said. She was still standing, and craned her neck to peer into the refrigerated case. The Germans had leaned their backpacks against the glass, obscuring the view of the sweets. The women, old but sturdy-looking, were talking very loudly.

She asked for an orange soda and sat down at one of the tables.

At first it had been the cockroaches. At night they came out of the drain in the sink and scuttled around in the kitchen and hall. Her book—a fictionalized biography of two British artists who, from the start of their careers, had lived together and created as if they were a single person—had been going well until one night she got up for a drink of water and saw a huge black cockroach wandering through the kitchen, its antennae swaying languidly. "Are you sure you can take care of yourself?" her boyfriend had asked on the phone. He wasn't just asking out of concern: the question hinted at his desire to come visit her on the island, a prospect the woman rejected immediately, since she was determined to avoid distractions during her stay. She went out and bought roach killer in both spray and powder form, emptied the cupboards, applied the stuff everywhere and in a few days the roaches were gone.

She had almost finished the first draft of her book when she got stuck on a single line. "We eat, we spit, we urinate, we defecate," one of the artists had said during an interview, and she wasn't sure if she should take it literally or as a somewhat cynical metaphor for the cycle of life. The fact that their final series had involved photographs of urine and sperm samples, magnified under a microscope, supported the second supposition but wasn't enough to resolve her doubts. She had seen the photographs; some of them showed fascinating shapes, exquisitely simple and original, like Paleolithic cave drawings. It was astonishing how much beauty there could be in strangers' revolting urine and sperm; she shivered in her chair at the thought, and new, more complex interpretations raced through her mind. She rose and was pacing rapidly up and down the room, trying to assess these new ideas, made dizzy by the possibilities opening up before her, when she noticed an equally beautiful shape, abstract and minimalist, on the floor in the hall. It took her five minutes to figure out it was a pile of mouse droppings.

The Germans were drinking their beers and singing, their faces bright red. I should say something to him, the woman thought, watching the waiter approach with her soda. Her nights had become nightmarish. She could hear the mice running through the kitchen and into her room, hiding under her bed, could feel them tugging at the sheets. It was impossible for her to concentrate. She had stopped writing. She tried all kinds of poisons, even the strongest; she cleaned out the cupboards and sprayed the whole house. Bizarrely, the mice devoured whatever she left out for them but only got fatter and stronger. They polished off a solution that contained enough strychnine to kill an army and came begging for more! She had caught one middle-aged mouse waiting for her to put out the poison, then pouncing on it like a junkie. The next morning it had stumbled out bleary-eyed to lick the same spot on the floor. The rodenticides also seemed to have an aphrodisiac effect: she had the impression that the mouse population was steadily increasing. The mice now roamed freely through the house even before it got dark, went on walks with their kids, had parties and invited friends from neighboring fields and barns.

"I need an exterminator," she said, and briefly told the waiter about the invasion of the mice. It was the first time she had asked for help from one of the locals—from the start she had tried to be self-sufficient, to write her book in isolation, avoiding contact with the villagers. But now, leaving the pastry shop with the exterminator's phone number scrawled on a napkin, she felt relieved, and as she walked through the fields on her way back to the house, some interesting ideas were starting to take shape about the two artists' apparent naiveté and the outrageous, almost blasphemous optimism that characterized their work. She couldn't wait to sit down at her table and write.

On the day the exterminator was to come, the woman put on a pair of jeans and a faded shirt, brushed her hair, and waited. It was early afternoon, much later than the time they had agreed on, when through the window she saw a middle-aged man slowly climbing the hill, a duffle bag and pump slung over his shoulder.

The exterminator surveyed the place. "No problem," he said, by which he presumably meant that the house was small and would be easy to fumigate. He was stout, with blue eyes and gentle features. He pulled a protective mask out of the duffle bag and put it on. The woman took a book and went outside. The sun was strong and she almost fell asleep listening to the crickets. When she opened her eyes, the air was cooler and the sun had sunk to the horizon.

The exterminator was washing his hands in the kitchen sink. There were puddles of a milky, phosphorescent liquid all over the house.

"Can I offer you a drink?" the woman asked after she paid him.

"Not on an empty stomach..."

"I'll cook something, we can eat together," she proposed, since she didn't much like the idea of being alone in the house and starting to discover the corpses of mice.

The exterminator accepted her invitation and the woman made a simple tomato sauce and boiled some pasta. It was a pleasure to watch him eat. He enjoyed every bite, taking great gulps of wine, and when he'd finished his third helping, he cleaned his plate carefully with identical chunks of fresh bread he had previously prepared. They hardly spoke. The exterminator ate, the woman watched him eat, and then he left, promising to come back the next day to check the results of the fumigation.

"I didn't see any corpses," the woman said the following afternoon. She was worried that the new poison might have become just another meal for the mice.

"You're lucky," said the exterminator, "you have the kind of mice that go elsewhere to die."

"Like elephants?"

The exterminator didn't reply. The woman noticed that he had showered and was wearing a clean shirt. Seeing him standing hesitantly in the doorway, she again suggested that he stay for lunch. She had chicken and potatoes in the oven and she made a big salad. Again she watched with interest the ritual of his meal, how he marked off the space around his plate, arranging his silverware and glass, tearing each slice of bread ahead of time into an equal number of pieces, and gently pushing his food around with his knife to create harmonious combinations. Then, finally, he started to eat, chewing slowly, thoughtfully, with unconcealed pleasure.

Over the next few days she made rapid progress on her book. She developed a new hypothesis about the urine samples that unfortunately didn't apply to the sperm. Not all secretions are waste. Nor can all theories be tailored to what we have in our heads, she had to admit. Even a man as ordinary as the exterminator couldn't be put in a mold. She knew very little about him. She encouraged him to talk about his life, but he never said much. When he was young he had worked for a carnival and had traveled all over Greece. He'd had a motorcycle and had ridden the Wall of Death. "It's a long story, full of passion and sorrow," he'd said, hunched over his plate.

He liked to eat. The taste of food drove him wild. He told her that at night he made the rounds of all the restaurants on the island that stayed open late, as ravenous as a beast. He works his way through his food the same way the mice did, the woman observed as for the fifth night in a row the exterminator sat down across the table from her and started to eat.

Until one night the exterminator said, "I'd like to taste something without swallowing." The woman looked at him quizzically and he kissed her. So they made love, and she discovered that he was the best lover she'd ever had. She hadn't had a chance to finish her meal, and when they got up out of bed, the exterminator went straight into the kitchen and cleaned her plate.

I think I'm in love, the woman thought. The next few days passed in a fever of cooking, sex, and writing. It was July, there was a heat wave and the wind blew off the sea in sudden gusts that singed your face, but nothing could stop the exterminator from climbing the hill to her house for food and sex. He was an incredible lover. He tried every spot on her body and devoted himself entirely to her desires, driving her to heights of ecstasy. And then, each night before he left, he would pump a bit of liquid rodenticide into all the corners of the house.

It was a glorious time. Her book was almost finished and showed extraordinary promise. She was usually modest, but she knew that when it was published it would leave everyone speechless, even the sternest critics. "I'm incredibly hungry, I'm hungry for French fries and an egg, over easy," the exterminator said that night. He had been licking the nipple of her left breast for a while, swallowing like a ruminant. Earlier, he had emptied a pan of stuffed peppers and a big bowl of Russian salad. "I'm hungry for French fries," he said sadly. He abandoned her nipple and began chewing the empty air. The woman got out of bed and went naked into the kitchen to make him what he wanted. "I'm so hungry it's driving me crazy," she heard him shout. "A real rib-eye steak," he groaned. The woman took a steak out of the freezer and put it under warm water to thaw.

How long had it been? Not long, though she was too emotional to note the time. As she was frying the potatoes and cracking the egg into hot oil, she felt her body rising with the steam. Carrying the tray into the bedroom, she bit into a crisp slice of potato and burned her tongue. She had never been so happy and nothing could have prepared her for the exterminator's death. She found him face up on the bed, his blue eyes open, his white belly swollen like a

"Sometimes I get crazy ideas," Stella was saying. "I think about throwing it all away and going off to Greece!" The prospect seemed so unlikely that she burst out laughing. She spit out her gum and skillfully twisted a hank of my hair around the circular brush. Then she switched on the dryer and trained its mouth on the curl of hair, scorching it with hot air. I felt like my earlobe was on fire, but didn't say anything.

We were in the bathroom of my room at the Del Capri Motel in Los Angeles, and Stella was doing my hair. She was a thin brunette with a pierced nose, a hairdresser who wanted to get into the movie business. "What would I do in Greece?" she asked, but didn't wait for a response. "I've never been there in my life. I don't know anyone over there." She laughed again, but her laugh—erratic, looping back on itself like a spring—was drowned out by the noise of the hair dryer.

Through the window I could see the atrium with its little heart-shaped pool, where a middle-aged woman was sunbathing on an inflatable crocodile; behind her, two palm trees stood motionless against the blue sky. I had checked into the Del Capri a few days earlier. It was a small hotel that looked like a cardboard cake wedged between glass apartment complexes and imposing office buildings. Everyone who worked there was somehow mixed up in the movies: the receptionist was a screenwriter, the guy who carried my bags was a sound technician, the maids were always going off to casting calls. When I asked where the closest hairdresser was, they said they'd have a girl come up to my room. "She's a director," they explained, then added, "and she's Greek."

I got up out of the chair and looked at myself in the mirror. On one side my hair was straight, flat against my head, cutting like a scythe under my chin; on the other side it stuck up in an unruly mess of colored clips and barrettes. "You'll see, it'll be fantastic," said Stella, spitting out another wad of gum. She took a fresh piece from her purse, unwrapped it, popped it in her mouth, then stuck the old piece in the empty wrapper. The hairdo was proceeding very slowly. Dryer off, dryer on. Burning of the ear. Changing of the gum. I asked if she knew people in Los Angeles, if she'd been able to do any networking. She said she'd met lots of important people, but her career had been almost entirely ruined because she'd fallen victim to a man who was practically a compatriot of ours, John Cassavetes. It was August of 1993; I told her Cassavetes had died in 1989. That was impossible, she said, because she'd seen him a few days earlier in front of Universal Studios. She stood thinking for a few minutes, then asked, "Who's the guy who made that movie about the woman who lives next door to the Satan worshippers and gets pregnant with Satan's child?"

"*Rosemary's Baby*?"

"Yeah, that one!"

"Roman Polanski."

"Yeah, him. He was living with Cassavetes and Ben Gazzara in this amazing villa in Beverly Hills. I'd gone there to figure out what was going on because they'd invited a friend of mine to a party and that night he disappeared. His mother kept calling me in tears every day, begging me to do something. So I went to look for him. They held me hostage in that villa for three months and tried to do the same thing to me. I got pregnant, just like that actress... like Mia Farrow."

"What happened to your friend?" I asked.

"He died," she answered, without explaining any further. I told her Roman Polanski had left the US in 1977 after a scandal that Jack Nicholson had also been involved in; he wasn't allowed back into the country, so there was no way he could have been in Beverly Hills during the time she was referring to. She didn't seem convinced. "He's a Satan worshipper," she said. "He can do whatever he wants, he could be in Europe and here at the same time if he wanted."

"And the baby?" I asked after a while.

"I aborted it in the bathtub. It hurt a lot." A shadow passed across her face. The memory seemed to upset her, but not for long. She pulled a can of hairspray from her purse and spritzed my hair, making an ardent cross in the air with the can as if blessing me. My cheeks started to tingle and I asked her what kind of hairspray she was using.

"Happy Hair," she said, then looked at me, surprised I hadn't heard of it. "It's what all the stars use."

She told me her parents had left their village in Greece when they were very young and had gotten married in the US. Her father had abandoned them after her younger sister was born. One morning when Stella was about twelve, her mother had dressed the girls in their best clothes and left for work. Two hours later the neighbors knocked on their door to tell them their mother had been killed in a car accident. Then came three years that Stella didn't remember at all. She figured she and her sister had been put in some kind of institution, but probably not together, because when they next saw one another, several years had passed and her sister had become a drug addict. After that Stella lost track of her. I asked her if she had any idea why her mother had dressed them in their best clothes that morning. "Because she knew she was going to die," she answered sharply, as if it were the most logical thing in the world. We tried to figure out what part of Greece her parents were from and finally decided—or I did—that it must have been Mani. It occurred to me that she might still have relatives there and that it might do her good to meet them, so I offered to try and track them down. The idea seemed to tempt her, but only briefly. "I don't have time," she murmured, "I'm so busy with the movies."

She bent over my head, frowning in consternation. Then she tousled my hair vigorously with her fingers and straightened it gently with her palms, so lightly she was barely touching it. "This one hair keeps getting away," she said, grabbing the hairspray and spritzing my hair and face before I could object. She looked at the results with satisfaction and switched on the dryer again. "I have absolute faith in Happy Hair," she declared cheerily. I said "happy hair" in Greek, "*eftihismena mallia,*" but she didn't seem to hear.

How long had she been in the institution? She couldn't remember. She wasn't even sure they'd put her in one, she might have stayed at the neighbors' house. She had a gap in her memory, a black trapdoor that swung open and stayed that way for three years. When her memory kicked in again, she was in a home for teens, training to be a hairdresser. Later she moved to New York, where she worked at Vidal Sassoon. She must have been eighteen when she decided to find her father. They met at a train station in some small city. It was winter, very cold, snowing. They fell into one another's arms, her father cried. He was a balding middle-aged man with playful eyes. "It just tore your heart out," Stella said, "to see those cheerful eyes overflowing with tears." He smelled like alcohol, but in a nice way, like liquor and cologne. He asked her forgiveness several times and promised he would never abandon her again. They stayed like that for a whole hour, hugging under the overhang at the station, while the snow came down around them. Everything was white, and the two of them a solitary black shape in a sea of ice. He invited her to spend Christmas with him and they said goodbye. When Stella called a few days later, a woman answered and swore at her. She tried once more, on Christmas Eve; the same woman answered, said her husband didn't have any daughters, and hung up on her. That was when Stella decided to move to the west coast and try to break into the movie business: with everything that had happened in her life, she figured the movies would fit her like a glove.

"I always get the craziest ideas when it's hot," Stella said. "I'm lying there in the sun and I suddenly feel so hopeless. I feel like throwing it all away, giving up the house and my job, giving up all my dreams, you know?" She spit out her gum, unwrapped a new piece and popped it in her mouth. She looked at me absentmindedly, the wad of gum in her hand. She couldn't find the new wrapper, so she stuck the chewed wad on the edge of the sink.

Stella had finished doing my hair and was getting ready to leave. We said a warm goodbye and made plans to get together that evening for a drink. I stayed at the hotel for a while, then went out. I was taking a walk through Venice Beach when I felt a strange tingling on my cheeks. Five minutes later, a rash had spread over my whole face, stinging horribly. Happy hair, indeed, I thought. I went into a drug store and bought a tube of cortisone cream. When I got back to the hotel, there was a message for me at the desk: *Can't make it tonight, meeting with important director. Love, Stella.*

In the bathroom mirror I saw an unfamiliar face, swollen, with sunken eyes. I rinsed it off several times, then bent down and let the water run over my head. Through that watery curtain, I saw a strange lump glowing on the edge of the sink: Stella's gum. I pulled it off and softened it between my fingers. It was green but smelled like strawberries.

A few months later, when I was back in Athens, I got a fax from Stella. She was writing to tell me how things were going, but the note was sort of disjointed and seemed more like a plea for help. I wrote back right away to say that if she decided to come to Greece she could stay with me for a while. There was no answer. I waited a few days and called. A recorded voice answered: subscriber unknown. I called the Del Capri. The staff had changed; no one there had ever heard of her.

September 3, 1969

It was nice today. I woke up late and went down to the harbor. The shops had closed for the afternoon and the streets were quiet. Not a leaf stirred. Only Mrs. Koula the bag lady was sitting on the steps of the church fanning herself with her hand. I kept going, onto the jetty, and sat at the coffee house to stare at the sea. Suddenly the heat dropped away and a gentle breeze began to blow. I ordered a beer and ate two tiropitakia. I got up and walked along the waterfront. I didn't see anyone I knew. A ship had just come in from Italy. It can't get into the harbor so it's waiting outside the breakwater, white and still. I heard they're putting the people in boats and ferrying them to the city.

On my way home in the afternoon I went through Psilalonia Square, then down Papaflessa Street. I passed by Hara's house. The shutters were closed today, too. They still haven't returned from vacation.

At home we had stuffed tomatoes and Sotiroula got mad because I ate the rice and left the tomatoes, which have vitamins, at the side of my plate, and I joked that if she kept talking about vitamins I would throw them all up. This evening I didn't do anything. Now I'm at home, in my room with the door closed. I'm looking through my father's old medical journals and wondering how the time is going to pass. My mother and Sotiroula are sitting on the balcony, talking. Maybe I'll go for a walk. Maybe I'll pass by her house again.

September 4, 1969
In the end I didn't do anything yesterday. I fell asleep in my clothes and when I woke up it was dawn and I was bathed in sweat. It was terribly hot. The heat didn't let up all day, and I had an awful headache that never went away.

September 6, 1969
Nothing today, either. Her shutters were closed, the house shut up as if they might never come back.

September 9, 1969
Today I met a classmate of hers, Maro. A strange creature, a little crazy, but she seems really smart. She can help me, I think. They're in the same class but not really friends. I was passing through Psilalonia and she was sitting with some guys who called me over to join them. I sat down and we started talking. As soon as she told me she goes to the Arsakeio girls' school, a sort of mania came over me and I told her everything. She looked at me kind of teasingly but maybe that's just what her eyes are like.

September 10, 1969
I saw the truck unloading outside her house and my heart felt like it would burst. The maid was running up and down giving orders to the movers. They'd even taken their beds and nightstands to the country. Eventually they started to unload all kinds of odds and ends, pots and pans

and kitchen things. Hara's mother came out onto the balcony in her robe and called to them to be careful, they were valuable objects, fragile. At some point I saw them take down a red bicycle that could've been hers—it's hers for sure, I thought, and for no reason I started to shake. Both tires were as flat as they could get. The mover was holding the bike under his arm and as he handed it to the maid, the handlebars hit the pavement and the bell gave out a weak little cry as if it were human. I jumped as if they'd caught me red-handed. I got mad at myself and came home.

September 18, 1969
Maro and I passed by her house. We walked up and down the street two or three times and then stood on the corner, behind the kiosk, and watched the front door. No one came out. Maro asked me for cigarettes and I bought her a pack. She smoked half the pack while we waited, putting out one and lighting another. She told me that Hara acts different in school now, that since the new school year started she seems kind of sad. "What do you think is going on?" I asked. "Her parents are strict, they're really hard on her and won't let her go out, her dad is a monster," she said. Hara's sister is two years older and goes to the Arsakeio, too, she's a senior, and a bitch, she treats Hara like dirt whenever they see each other during break, and she's going out with a university student from Athens, only no one knows. That's what I found out. In Maro's opinion, the sister is the biggest obstacle.

No one came out of the house. The windows and balcony doors on the second floor were closed. But if you looked more carefully you could see that the shutters were open just a tiny bit, and through the crack you could make out the green latch and then deep darkness. "You think Hara is standing there, watching us?" I asked Maro and she laughed.

It was getting late. Maro told me that Hara's mother is sick all the time, she gets migraines and hardly ever leaves the house. At ten at night we decided to leave. We went to Omonia for souvlaki. "You need to come out into the light," Maro said suddenly. I looked at her questioningly. "You have to write her a letter." We agreed that she'll write it because she has more ideas and knows Hara better, and she'll give it to me to copy and then take it to Hara.

September 19, 1969
Maro gave me the letter. I almost had a stroke.

> *Present tense*
> I love
> you love
> he/she/it loves
> we love
> you all love
> they love
>
> *Simple past*
> I loved
> you loved

he/she/it loved
we loved
you all loved
they loved

Continuous past
I was loving
you were loving
he/she/it was loving
we were loving
you all were loving
they were loving

Etc. etc. It was all there. Even the past perfect and the passive voice. "Are you messing with me?" I asked. "What do you want to write, 'my darling' and all that crap?" Maro said contemptuously. "This says it all! That's how you'll convince her," she said. She left the letter with me and walked off.

Maybe she's right. I went home, shut myself in my room and wrote the verb love in all its tenses. Maybe Maro is right—I have to impress Hara because I'm older, I went to Italy to study medicine, then gave it all up and came back, so obviously I can't write like a schoolboy. I have to send her something unusual, something unique. I have to startle her.

September 21, 1969
All day today I waited for Maro. Since yesterday when I gave her the letter she's nowhere to be found. I called her

house three times but a younger kid answered, probably her brother, and said she was out. I can't sit still. My nerves are shot. I went down Papaflessa but didn't dare go anywhere near Hara's house because I didn't know if she'd gotten my letter. If she had and I ran into her, what would I do? Would I talk to her? She might pretend not to know who I was. She has to give the first sign, smile at me or turn to look at me, encourage me in some way. I can't do anything since I don't know what's happened. I have to wait for Maro. I can't stand it anymore. I feel like the walls of my room are going to fall in and crush me.

September 22, 1969
I finally saw Maro. She was in Psilalonia, sitting and smoking on the steps in front of the statue of Bishop Germanos. She told me her parents had taken her to a psychiatrist in Athens. At first I didn't believe her. I looked at her suspiciously. "I'm not kidding," she said.

She told me she'd given Hara the letter but didn't know how she'd taken it, she'd tell me tomorrow. Tomorrow, tomorrow, how am I going to live until tomorrow.

December 19, 1969
Today I couldn't get out of bed. Sotiroula knocked on my door and told me to get up and help her decorate the Christmas tree. I swore at her, went back to sleep and woke up at three in the afternoon. I went for coffee in Psilalonia. I wasn't thinking about anything at all until I

saw Maro from a distance sitting next to the statue of Bishop Germanos and smoking. She spoiled my mood. I got up and left the coffee shop before she could see me. I don't want to hear her explanations again. I don't want her to tell me all the same things with that teasing look of hers, that Hara's a hard case, that we have to write her another letter, more revolutionary...

December 25, 1969
Awful day. It's been raining since morning.

January 20, 1970
My mother came into my room and told me to get my papers ready, to see if we could get my grades from Italy transferred. I started shouting. I told her I don't care, she should leave me alone, and she gave me a look like a whipped dog. Then she went in and yelled at Sotiroula, who bore the brunt of it in the end.

Today, for the first time in a long time, I went down Papaflessa Street. I stood behind the kiosk, in the same spot where Maro and I waited back in September. It was freezing. Hara's father came hurrying up to the house at one-thirty and left again at three. He seemed out of sorts, in a bad mood. A while later their maid came out and headed toward the kiosk. I ran to hide. She started talking to the man at the kiosk. When she left, I went back to my spot. It was almost dark when I saw Hara's sister come out and close the door behind her carefully as if she didn't want to be heard. She stood on the front step and looked down the street in both directions. She went down the stairs and walked off. I followed her. As soon as she turned the corner she started to run. I ran after her. She headed up toward Trion Navarhon Street. For a while I thought I'd lost her but then I caught sight of her blond ponytail bobbing in the darkness. I hurried to catch up.

What I saw was terrible. Under the marble steps, in that archway, a man with very dark skin was waiting, hidden behind the dense foliage. I couldn't see him very well but he looked about thirty, he couldn't have been the student Maro told me about. They didn't say anything, Hara's sister just fell into his arms and they started kissing passionately. He put his hands under her coat and pulled up her skirt. I heard them grunting and groaning. I felt horribly agitated, the blood rushed to my head and I left, stumbling backwards.

February 2, 1970
Sotiroula woke me up at the crack of dawn to tell me I had a phone call. It was Maro. I hadn't heard her voice in a while and didn't recognize it. "I'm calling from a kiosk," she said, out of breath, "they're taking us on a field trip to the forest, you should come, it's your last chance." In a daze, I washed up, got dressed and went down to hail a cab. As it wound its way up into the hills I was overcome by doubt. Why was I getting involved with Maro again? And what if today brought the knockout blow?

When I got there I saw that the whole school had

come up to the forest and the girls had scattered in little groups. Maro was waiting for me on the road, hiding behind a bulldozer, as she'd said she would. Hide, hide, she gestured to me, and I went and stood behind a barrel of tar. She told me to head up the road that went toward the castle and when I saw the first bench, to turn right and start going down into the forest. I should walk about fifty meters in and wait there.

I don't know how long I waited. I could hear the girls' voices and laughter from a distance and every so often the teacher's whistle. My feet were stone cold and I stomped on the ground to keep them from going numb, and then for a while it seemed absolutely silent, as if the field trip were over and the girls had left. At some point I heard footsteps, branches creaking. Hara was coming toward me. I'm dreaming, I thought when I saw her. But it was Hara, and she was alone.

From up close she was even more beautiful.

From up close her eyes were amazing.

From up close her mouth was pink, her lips full and slightly parted, a tiny little tooth shone like a pearl.

"Hi, Hara," I said and it seemed as if someone else were speaking, that's how calm I was.

She looked at me silently. She was wearing a coat over her uniform and had her hands in her pockets.

"How are you?" I asked.

For an instant she wavered, shifting her weight to her left leg. I smiled and stepped toward her. Suddenly she turned and ran for the road. I froze where I was, unable to react.

When I finally found my strength and started to walk, I headed back up to the road. The girls had lined up in threes and were starting to move off. They were singing but I couldn't make out the words. Maro had stayed behind, by the bulldozer. She had something black in her hands and I realized she was playing with the tar as if it were plasticine. What happened? she asked with her eyes. I didn't feel like talking to her. I saw her put a piece of tar in her mouth and start to chew, staring at me with that strange look of hers.

February 22, 1970
This is going to be the worst Carnival of my life.

February 28, 1970
I counted two men in drag, a cowboy, a marquise and a caveman who I then realized was actually a beggar. They passed Hara's house and headed toward the central square, dancing clumsily.

March 2, 1970
"Have you ever gone to the Black Domino ball?" Maro asked. I said no. "There are orgies," she said and described some incredible scenes that I bet she was just making up. I knew she was trying to get me to go with her but I wasn't going to get myself into that kind of mess.

In the end we went. Maro rented a black domino robe,

or rather I rented it and she went into the restroom of a souvlaki place to change. When she came out I didn't recognize her. "Psst, psst," she said, and I knew who she was from the sound of her voice. "Dominoes aren't supposed to speak, so no one will recognize them," she told me. We went to the box office at the theater. A middle-aged woman was sitting behind the glass and told us that men needed tickets but women got in free. If anyone finds out I went to the domino ball with a schoolgirl I'm finished, I thought as we went in. It was afternoon but the theater was packed. The band on the stage was playing a cha-cha and the whole place was bouncing up and down to the music. In one of the theater boxes I saw some friends of my father's who I'd thought had died. They were wearing suits, each one dancing with two dominoes.

I lost sight of Maro and found myself alone in the wild crowd. All the women looked alike in their black dresses, gloves and masks. They put their arms around me and pulled me by the neck to dance. "Is it you?" I asked every now and then to find out if it was Maro but the women just cackled.

I went out of the ballroom and sat down on the stairs in the lobby. Piles of streamers overflowed down the stairs. I was sweating and my ears were ringing from all the noise. What if Hara is hiding behind one of those masks? I wondered and for a while I imagined the scene: a domino pulling me by the hand, us climbing the stairs arm in arm and going into one of the boxes, her taking off the mask... Those bright eyes, those pink lips. But that would never happen. "Psst, psst." Maro had come up without my recognizing her. "I figured out how the next letter should start," she said, excited. "Forget it," I said, standing up. "I was an emir of good luck and became an unlucky one," Maro sang in a falsetto and then started to laugh as if she was possessed. I told her I wanted to leave and pulled her roughly outside.

March 8, 1970
It rained the whole time the floats were going by. I didn't feel like watching the parade but unfortunately I had gotten tangled in Maro's nets again. She called me to say that Hara and her parents were going to some family friend's house to watch the Carnival King parade and she suggested that we go too and wait downstairs. Her plan was to go inside at some point and tell Hara to come out so we could talk. Nothing happened. The road was closed, people were pushing and shoving and we didn't even get to the front door of the building where Hara supposedly was.

We got soaked. At seven when the rain stopped, people started heading to the harbor to watch them burn the Carnival King. The square filled with trash, trampled streamers and cotillions in muddy water. We walked aimlessly under the arcades and Maro asked me to buy her a cognac. Cognac? I was speechless, but I did what she wanted. Then we went toward the church of Agios Andreas. It was deserted everywhere. We could hear the fireworks from far off and the sky over the harbor was on fire.

We walked into the little park by the sea and Maro was making strange sounds with her mouth. "What are

There were two pills inside. "Take one," she said. I didn't want to. "It's Largactil, it's really great," she insisted. I didn't want to take it but something like inertia came over me and I did, and because I couldn't swallow it without water we went into a sweet shop and Maro made me buy her a touloumba and bit off the end, then gave me the rest because she doesn't like sweets. At first everything was normal. As we were walking it seemed like my feet were rising a little higher than they should off the ground, but probably I was doing it myself, and every time we crossed the street and went up onto the sidewalk I bent my knees high. Maro indifferent at my side as if nothing was wrong. A while later I felt like I was floating. Everything gray and a little cloud in my head. We'd crossed the entire city, climbed up to the castle, gone back down the other side, and then toward the old port, but I wasn't tired at all, my body was moving on its own, I didn't have to make any effort. "Let's go see a friend of mine," Maro said. Her friend had been hit by a car the night before and was in a clinic. It was a little building behind the customs office and her friend's room was on the second floor. One of her legs was hanging from the ceiling in a cast, her left arm was in a cast too, her whole head was wrapped up like a mummy's in gauze with dried blood on it. But she seemed to be in a great mood. There was a little transistor radio on the bedside table playing *"If it were 1821, if I could go back just for a night..."* at full blast. Maro sat on the bed at the girl's feet and they talked, or rather Maro talked and the girl nodded her head because she couldn't move her mouth. I was standing and listening to various sounds in my head.

"Great, I'll kiss the wall!" Maro suddenly said and jumped up from the bed. The girl nodded in agreement. I was absorbed in the sounds and it took me a while to realize what was happening. Maro pushed me onto the bed and went and stood facing the wall. "For as long as I'm kissing the wall, you guys have to kiss," she said. I bent over the girl and touched her lips with mine. *"I'd ride over the wide threshing floor, and with Kolokotronis..."* is all I remember because the transistor kept playing the same song.

We went outside, it had started to rain and Maro seemed very happy, her eyes were shining. We walked hand in hand through the dark streets and when we reached the lights we ran until we were out of breath. I felt carefree, too. The few passersby gave us questioning looks but we didn't care. The rain fell harder and we played hopscotch in the square. "If it were 1821," I sang in a shrill voice. "With General Pattakos in my arms..." Maro sang back, off key, I gestured for her not to overdo it, and just then noticed four umbrellas coming toward us, crossing the square. They passed by us like shadows and moved off, walking faster. Underneath the umbrellas were Hara and her parents and sister.

That was the end. I'm home now, shut up in my room. Never, never again. I'll never forget the contempt in Hara's eyes. That was the pinnacle of my humiliation.

June 18, 1970
Leaving Patra was the right thing to do. That place had made me sick. I've been calmer since I came to Athens.

Who cares if my mother says I'm digging her grave.

November 8, 1974
It's been a long time. Today as I was reading this diary it seemed as if someone else had written it. There are some things I'd forgotten entirely, like Maro eating tar on the trip to the forest, or that the mover had dropped Hara's bike and it made a human noise and I got scared.

June 21, 1976
It's okay that she got married. Maybe it's better this way. Maybe now she'll be less afraid and won't avoid me. She'll feel like there's some certainty in her life. And who knows? Maybe at some point she'll agree to meet me.

July 3, 1976
I blew it. I drank two whiskeys and called her. No one answered. I called again and lay down on the sofa as the phone rang in an empty apartment. I counted six rings, lying motionless with my eyes closed.

I went into the kitchen, ate a spoonful of honey and gargled with warm water. I sat at the table and wrote down what I would say to her if she answered. I corrected it and copied it out again. I read it out loud, practicing so I would sound natural: "Hi… I don't know if you remember me, I'm…" My voice was hoarse and distorted, the voice of a drunken hippopotamus.

No one was home. They must both work. A young couple—though from what I've been told he's not so young anymore. They leave early for work and don't see one another until evening. They cook together in the kitchen. They laugh and talk about how their days went. Maybe he opens a bottle of red wine and offers her a glass. Their house is spare, but with nice plates and napkins.

November 14, 1976
I went to a fortune teller. I paid two thousand drachmas to hear that Hara is going to get a divorce in three weeks, or three months, or three years, and then we'll get married… Shame on me!

March 9, 1977
Enough. I have to put an end to this. I've become a caricature of myself.

February 11, 1980
I feel worse every day. Every day I hope will be the last. Today an acquaintance from Patra came to see me. He wanted to meet somewhere for coffee but I told him to come by the house. It surprised him to see that I was so fat, everyone thinks sick people are skinny. He brought me news from home but I couldn't follow what he was saying. The poor guy thought it would cheer me up to hear some gossip about life in the provinces. I did learn, though, that Hara

and her husband got a divorce, and now they're fighting over the kid in court. "Do you remember that lunatic, Maro?" he asked at some point. "She's a lawyer now, a big shot, she even opened her own office in London! Who ever would have guessed, from that wreck…"

That snapped me out of my lethargy and I started asking him questions. He told me all sorts of things, it made my head spin, who died, who divorced, who married whom. I asked what had happened to that friend of Maro's who'd been hit by the car. "You didn't hear? Kaput," he said. "As soon as she got out of the clinic and could walk again, she took her father's car and drove it into the sea. She was all bloated when they found her."

Of all the things he told me, that upset me the most. Because deep down my memories of that time aren't bad. I remember everything and everyone with affection. And that story that started like a nice dream and turned into a bad joke, when I think of it now it seems like a happy time. Of course there are moments when I sink into a horrible despair.

October 1, 1985
In a cab I suddenly remembered her kiss. I was on my way home from the doctor's, we were going down Zoodohou Pigis, about to turn onto Akadimias. I remembered the girl's head wrapped in gauze, a fleeting but powerful image. I remembered the dried blood, her leg hanging from the ceiling, her arm in the cast. I remembered my face approaching hers, her yellow eyes, that feverish gaze,

my lips touching hers. I felt an awful fear. I leaned back in the seat and listened to my heart beating.

October 4, 1985
I dreamed that we were going to meet. I had come home from Italy, I was still a student. I gathered my courage and finally decided to talk to her. We met in a coffee shop that was like a dive bar, there were other people there, too, but I don't remember their faces. "I love you very much," I told her, "please give me a chance." She looked at me as if she didn't understand. "All I'm asking for is a chance," I begged. "I'll think about it," she said, "you have to wait, I'll give you an answer in a week." How did that week pass? In my dream I lived each day separately from morning until night, then until the next morning, too— hours of agitation, anguish and expectation. But I didn't despair, the mere fact that she had agreed to think it over gave me hope. We met so she could tell me what she had decided. We started to talk. And then I suddenly realized it wasn't her but Maro. I don't know if she had been Maro from the beginning, from our first meeting at the bar, or if she only turned into Maro later on. The fact is, I realized Hara was Maro and woke up.

October 13, 1985
This house is too small, I know it inside out. I know its every spot, its most secret corners. Sometimes I seem to see her coming down the hall with a flower in her hand.

"A flower for me?" I ask. She looks at me sadly. And I start to laugh.

October 16, 1985
Today, on the sixteenth of October, at seven in the evening, as I was about to open a can of tuna, I heard a hammering in my ear, something knocked three times and then stopped. I jumped up right away.

I ran into the bathroom. I couldn't find a razor in the medicine cabinet, or anywhere else. I bit my hand until it bled. Then I tore off my shirt, wrapped it around my neck and tried to strangle myself. I stood on a stool and started to pound my head against the mirror.

Now it's night, I've put everything in order, I cleaned up the broken glass, the shards of the mirror, and ate some tuna salad. The TV is on with no sound. I'm terribly calm and determined. I've never been so at peace. I've never felt this sweet shiver down to the bone, this gentle numbness that paralyzes my limbs as I slip into a deep sleep. Good night, my little Hara, good night, Maro, good night.

aren't you going to walk the dog?

The street in front of the theater was deserted and a cold wind was blowing. "Wasn't that fun?" the daughter asked, and hugged the mother. The daughter was much taller, and the mother instinctively drew back. The movie had been so-so, not bad, just indifferent, and though it had starred her favorite actor, an actor she'd been crazy about in her youth, the mother was certain that in a few days she'd have forgotten the plot.

"You're so tiny," the daughter said. "It makes me want to squeeze you!"

Al Pacino's really aged, the mother thought. If I had the opportunity to meet him now, I'm not sure I'd be interested. She remembered him in *Scarface*, and before that in *Dog Day Afternoon*—she'd adored him in that, for his intense, passionate look, and because he wasn't handsome in the classical sense, because her girlfriends didn't like him—and she remembered herself twenty years ago, on the balcony of the Excelsior theater in Florence, watching the movie for the third time and eating a Penguin ice cream cone.

"Mom, did you just yawn? Don't do that, it makes tears run down your face and you look awful."

"Okay."

They walked arm in arm, glued to one another. Hardly any cars passed in the street. The shop windows were lit up. A taxi stopped short, then followed alongside them for a few meters. The driver rolled down the passenger's-side window and muttered something through his teeth, or so it seemed to the mother. Then the taxi, a Mercedes, sped up and disappeared. They reached a corner and crossed to the opposite sidewalk. There was that hideous store that sold mirrors and bathroom accessories; it took up half the block and looked like a brightly lit shack. A bit further on the guy at the neighborhood's only kiosk was lowering the grates, and the mother wondered if she should run and buy cigarettes. She caught a brief glimpse of herself beside her daughter in one of the shop's mirrors. Her body looked square. With skinny little chopstick legs. Like a hobgoblin, she thought.

"Mom, are you deaf?" the daughter said.

"Did you say something?" the mother asked.

The daughter didn't reply. She pulled her cell phone out of her pocket and checked to see if she had any messages, put the phone back and passed an arm through the mother's, clinging to her tightly. They walked to the next corner, then turned right and took a shortcut across the deserted square. Trash and empty boxes blocked the entrance to an abandoned theater. The title on the marquee was torn and hung down over a pile of canvas that was curled up like a human body, and the mother strained her neck to read the letters: NEVER SPEAK... Something furry, maybe a rat, jumped out from the trash and scurried into the middle of the road. NEVER SPEAK OF ROPE... She couldn't read the rest.

Home at last, the mother thought as she unlocked the door to the building. She'd had a vague headache, a kind of pressure behind her eyes, the whole way home, and now as she opened the door to the apartment and stepped into the bright room with the shiny parquet and the dog jumping at her legs, she felt relieved. She'd left all the lights on, she had forgotten that. The TV was on, too, she could hear the tinny voice of some talk show host. "I thought I turned everything off," she said.

The daughter took off her jacket and hurried into her room.

The mother stopped in the middle of the hall. "Aren't you going to walk the dog?" she asked to her daughter's back. She heard the door close and the key turn in the lock.

The mother went into the kitchen and looked at the dirty dishes in the sink. She chose a glass from the pile, rinsed it out and filled it with water. Glass in hand, she opened the fridge and looked in. There were lots of things she could eat and for a moment she wavered between a cold chicken sandwich with mustard and a stuffed tomato left over from the day before. Out the corner of her eye she saw the dog watching her, wagging his tail. "Calm," she said. She set the glass on the counter and leaned into the fridge so she could see better. She looked again at the dog. He hadn't moved from his spot but his tail was going back and forth like a metronome. "Calm!" she said again and realized she had raised her voice.

She closed the fridge, left the kitchen, went and stood outside the daughter's room. Confused sounds were coming from inside, drums and flutes and a hypnotized male voice that repeated the same phrase over and over, then screamed as if he were swallowing razor blades. She took a step closer and knocked on the door.

"Aren't you going to walk the dog?" she asked in a strained voice.

"Leave me alone, I can't stand you," the daughter shouted, turning up the music.

The mother grabbed the doorknob and shook it. Then she kicked the door.

"Mom, are you insane?" the daughter asked from inside the room. There was a thump and approaching footsteps, then the music got even louder and the man's voice came back, subterranean and threatening.

The mother leaned her back against the door. Her heart was pounding irregularly and her foot hurt from the kick. "Come here, Max," she said to the dog, who came over obediently. "You're stupid, you know that?" she whispered and as the dog stared at her with the same sad expression, she wondered if it would make her feel better to kick him too, to give him a good hard kick between the legs. I'm losing it, she thought, and bolted back to the kitchen.

She picked up the glass of water and drank it down. She set the empty glass on the counter and squeezed it as hard as she could. Her skin went red at the knuckles and her fingers started to turn white. I have to apologize, she thought, and for a few minutes she stood there motionless, staring at the tiles in front of her. The wall, the tiles, the shelf of cookbooks, everything was in its place, and that infuriated her even more; for some reason it made her feel helpless. I definitely have to apologize, she thought again. Tears burned the corners of her eyes. Don't do this to me, she told herself. Not that kitchen melodrama again. Scenes from movies came to mind, the heroine, drunk, crying alone by the sink, Jack Nicholson and Jessica Lange making love on the kitchen table, Al Pacino in a white apron in *Frankie and Johnnie*, fixing Michelle Pfeiffer something special, then offering it to her with shining eyes. That fiery look, full of expectation. Everything could change if I wanted it to, she thought. Tonight could develop into something exceptional. I could fill the tub with hot water and take a bubble bath. I could make an amatriciana and eat watching a movie on TV. I should walk the dog first so afterward I can relax. I'll take him out when the water boils, she decided.

She took out a pot, filled it with water and set it on the burner. She chose two cloves of garlic and chopped them finely, carefully removing the little green tail. She measured six spoons of olive oil into a pan, which she set on another burner. Why amatriciana? she wondered, standing there with the wooden spoon in her hand. Why not carbonara? Why not pomarola, a plain tomato sauce, simple but delicious? She felt distressingly suspended between these choices, and at the same time was afraid her anger might return. "What do you think?" she asked the dog, who wagged his tail half-heartedly. The die is cast, amatriciana it is, she said to herself. She took the jar of chilies from the cupboard, picked out two and crumbled them into the pan where the garlic was browning, then licked her finger and felt the burn.

"What are you making, Mom?" The daughter was standing in the doorway. Leaning on the doorframe, her face half in light and half in shadow, she was so beautiful, an extraordinary creature, irresistible.

"Amatriciana," the mother said, and felt herself drowning in joy at the sight of those gorgeous lips, those radiant teeth.

"Nice," her daughter said, then lowered her eyes. "I wanted to ask you something," she mumbled.

"What?" the mother asked, still entranced. She turned around and stirred the garlic with the wooden spoon. Now is when I should apologize, she thought.

"Please don't say no," the daughter burst out.

"What do you want?"

"Promise me you won't say no!" the daughter insisted to her back.

The mother turned and looked at her. The daughter was holding her cell phone out in her right hand. "I just got a text," she said excitedly. "Everyone's going to a club. Everyone! Can I go, please?"

"Absolutely not," the mother said.

"I'm begging you."

"I don't want you wandering around at night."

"Please, I'm begging you. Please."

The mother made no reply. She opened the can of tomatoes and dumped them into the pan, then stirred quickly. "It's boiling," she murmured, looking at the water in the pot. She knew the daughter was still standing behind her, waiting. She opened the cupboard, took out a box of spaghetti, and emptied it into the hot water. Why insist? she wondered. It was pointless, since eventually she would give in. She would give in as she always did.

"Are you coming to eat?" she asked a while later, her face lost in steam.

"Shit, forget it," the daughter said, and left the room.

"Come here, sweet girl," the mother whispered. It was after midnight and she was sitting alone at the kitchen table. She had eaten a forkful of spaghetti straight from the pot and drunk some whiskey and now she could feel the alcohol affecting her, her limbs starting to go numb. The evening had been an avalanche of mistakes: the daughter had left without her permission, the pasta had turned to mush, the dog was still waiting for his walk. She had sent two text messages, but there had been no response. She stared at her cell phone beside the pack of cigarettes as if waiting for salvation, as if she could make it ring just by looking at it long and hard enough. Why did she do this to me? she thought. Why did she leave when she knew I'd let her go in the end?

She took the bottle down off the shelf and poured herself some more whiskey. She noticed that the bread box on the counter was ajar, a loaf of bread inside. She got up and opened the lid. The loaf hadn't been touched and was deathly white, the crust yellowish at the corners. She remembered having gone shopping that morning, but didn't remember buying bread, not that *particular* loaf. She ran a finger over its surface, which was cold and slightly sweaty. "What's happening to me?" she asked out loud. Everything was wrong. Everything was against her. She closed the bread box and started to cry.

There was a creak, a window opening. Someone on the floor below stuck his head out and spat into the air shaft. The radiators gurgled and fell silent. Then the dog came into the kitchen and barked. The mother sat back down at the table. Tears running down her cheeks, she picked up her cell phone and looked at it. No messages. She pushed back her chair and stood up. She went into the hall and put the leash on the dog. She shrugged on her coat and put her keys and cigarettes in one pocket. As she was locking the door behind her, she heard the radiators gurgling again and realized she had forgotten her phone. She unlocked the door, went into the kitchen, picked it up from the table and went back out. In the elevator the dog started squirming and jumping. The mother wiped away her tears and gripped the leash as tightly as she could, close to her body. As they went out into the street, the dog charged forward. She staggered after him and started to run, her arm outstretched.

Before them stood the silent mass of the church with its pillars and marble lions. The square was deserted. Two stray dogs were fighting in the courtyard. The mother tried to pull the leash toward her, but the dog, stretching his neck muscles and sticking out his chest, continued on unfazed, dragging her along. Her hair blew and the icy wind hit her face. We're running, she thought, I'm drunk and we're running. The church's four pillars, the two dogs, one red and one brown, the statue, the little park behind it, the whole perimeter of the square were passing frame by frame out the corner of her eye, and she was out of breath. It seemed to her that the strays were trying to fuck in front of the church door, and that in the distance the old deaconess was limping toward them with her cane.

Suddenly the dog stopped. The mother stopped, too, breathing hard. She was sweating and she unbuttoned her coat. The dog stuck his nose into a bag of scraps and started to eat. The mother took her phone out of her pocket and checked the screen. No messages. "Come on, Max," she said. She tugged at the leash and they started walking, into the little park. It was very dark there. The wind had died down and it was completely silent. "Aren't you ashamed of yourself, Max?" she said, and the dog looked up at her, the dismembered bag in his jaws.

They walked along the edge of the railing beside the flower beds. A few steps further on was a bench. They wandered around for a while, then the mother sat down on the bench and let the dog off the leash. The tears had dried on her face and her skin felt taut and pinched. How dark the park was at that spot! The trees seemed to be wrapped in murky webs, the leaves were dull and opaque, every now and then a piece of trash shone like a firefly against the black earth. She remembered a poem she used to like, back when she was in love with Al Pacino. "The World of Colors," by Yevtushenko. *When I met you began for me the world of colors...* Maybe it wasn't by Yevtushenko. Or maybe it was some other poem. She tried to remember how it went. She felt something stirring inside her, the shiver of a youthful love. "When I met you..." she whispered.

can anybody hear me?

Galina Petrova was walking to work under the weight of a humid, suffocating heat. There were only two blocks to go but she had started dragging her feet. She stopped at the kiosk on the corner to catch her breath and drank from her water bottle. She thought of the conversation she'd had that morning with her husband, Liosha, and instinctively bit her lip. *That's how birds make their nests, by stealing. Well, we're birds, too.* Those had been his exact words. Exhausted, she crossed the street. The building, a freshly painted corner property, stood out from the rest of the houses, with their low roofs and vine-covered terraces. As she approached, she noticed Nelly standing motionless at one of the windows on the third floor. There was something so distressing about that motionlessness, something that oppressed Galina, though she didn't know why.

That summer Nelly was as white as milk and hadn't grown so much as a centimeter. Her face had shrunk and her eyes were sunken. Her elbows and knees were red and chapped, as if she had scraped them against stone. Nelly had stopped leaving the house the previous autumn. She was afraid of slipping off the earth and falling.

"Falling where?" her girlfriends would ask when they came to see her—every day during the first week, then less and less frequently.

Nelly had no response. Face down on her bed, she gripped the bedframe and stared at them.

"I want my daughter back," the mistress would whisper into the phone.

Ever since Nelly got sick, Galina had been working double shifts. She came at eight in the morning and left at nine at night. Sometimes, when the mistress needed her, she didn't go home at all, but slept in the little room next to the kitchen. At first Liosha complained, but he soon got used to the new arrangement. With the extra money he could buy as much beer as he wanted, by April he was bargaining for cars, and in June he managed to buy a little used Fiat.

"Good morning, Galina," said the mistress, who was already dressed in a pair of white slacks and a yellow blouse. Smoking, she repeated the same things she had told Galina the day before—instructions about Nelly, her medication, the drops at precisely seven p.m.

"Got it?" she sighed in closing.

"Yes," Galina said. But her mind was elsewhere; she was thinking of Liosha and his tricks.

"The doctor will be here at two," the mistress said. "Ask if he wants coffee."

Nelly had spent the winter and spring in the clinic, and though she'd been able to get out of bed and wander from room to room since early June, she still never went outside.

"Be careful, Galina, okay?"

Galina nodded.

A suitcase was yawning open on the armchair in the bedroom, and some clothes were neatly folded beside the pillow. The mistress picked up her make-up bag, unzipped it and stuck in a bottle of sunscreen. Then she opened the wardrobe, rummaged through the drawers and took out two bathing suits.

"Do you need me for anything else?" Galina asked, turning to leave.

"Nelly's in the living room," the mistress said. "Please, keep an eye on her…"

"I'll make her burgers," Galina said.

The mistress turned and looked at her as if trying to guess what she was thinking. "It's a very important meeting," she said. "Otherwise I wouldn't leave."

"I'll take care of her."

They were standing in the foyer in front of the open door. Mr. Tsirimokos, their neighbor, appeared in the hall, dragging a cart full of groceries. "Going on vacation?" he asked.

"I wish," the mistress said, her tone a little sour. Then she smiled. "A business trip, I'm afraid… but I'll try to find time for a swim."

The morning passed quickly. Galina cleaned the house with the radio on, opening the door to the living room every so often to see what Nelly was doing. She was always standing in the same position in front of the window.

At one the phone rang. It was Liosha. "I think I'll come over," he said.

"I'll lose my job," Galina told him.

Liosha laughed, then fell silent. Galina could picture

him with his feet up on the kitchen table, beer in hand.

"Talk to you later," he said and hung up.

Galina wiped her hands on her apron and looked down the hall at the floor gleaming in the afternoon light. She opened the door to the living room and went over to Nelly.

"What are you looking at?" she asked.

"The nest," Nelly said, and Galina followed her gaze. Outside, stuck to the balcony wall, was a long, narrow, funnel-shaped nest made of mud. "I've been watching it for three hours and nothing's happened."

Just then a big bird flew up, chirping. It circled the nest a few times and left.

"Like what?"

"There are no baby birds."

"They must be sleeping," said Galina.

"The big bird killed them," Nelly said.

The big bird had come back. In its beak was a sliver of wood, which it was trying to press into the mud of the nest. As soon as the wood stuck the bird flew off.

"It's been doing that all day," Nelly said, then looked at Galina, waiting for a response.

The nest appeared to be completely sealed, without any kind of opening, not even a little hole to let the air in.

"That nest is a tomb," Nelly said.

Galina couldn't think of anything worth saying. She went into the hall, where the phone was. She dialed her number and let the phone ring several times. No one answered. Liosha must already have left.

At two the doctor came, the one Nelly called Sparrownose. He was sweaty and complained of the heat. "Very hot," Galina echoed and went into the kitchen. When she came back into the living room with a tray of coffee and cookies, the doctor was standing behind the desk and Nelly was sitting across from him. Her face was pale and strained. The doctor motioned for Galina to wait.

"The earth is turning," Nelly was saying, "and we're stuck to it and we have to hold on so we don't fall… like terrified ants…"

"Okay," Sparrownose broke in. He glanced absent-mindedly out the window and sat down in the armchair. "So, it seems we've been holding on tight for… five, six thousand years…"

"Ten thousand," said Nelly.

"Ten!" Sparrownose exclaimed. "Just imagine—ten thousand years, and not a single one of us has fallen yet!"

But that wasn't proof enough for Nelly, who stood up in a huff and went over to the window. Galina took the opportunity to set the tray down on the desk and leave.

At lunchtime Nelly didn't want to eat. Galina made her French fries, a cheese omelet, a hamburger. "Eat, little bird," she said. Nelly pushed her plate away and got up. "I'm tired," she said, and went to her room.

It must have been past six when Galina heard the doorbell. The living room was boiling in the late afternoon sun and she was bathed in sweat. Liosha was leaning against the door frame, a broad smile on his face. "You shouldn't have come," Galina said. She looked over to make sure the neighbor's door was closed, then stepped aside to let him in.

"It's hot out," he said, and went into the kitchen. He had been to the house once before, when Nelly was in the clinic and the mistress was still spending her nights there. It had been winter, and he and Galina had slept in one another's arms and made love in the mistress's bed, despite Galina's protests. In the morning she fried him some eggs, sunny side up, and they ate naked in bed, the tray resting on the covers. But that had been a different Liosha, a calmer, more reasonable Liosha who only drank on the weekends, not every day.

"There are leftover hamburgers," Galina said.

"Hamburgers again?" he asked, raising his voice.

"The girl is sleeping," Galina said.

"I don't give a shit about the girl," Liosha grunted. He sat down at the table, lit a cigarette and looked around. "Nice," he said, exhaling smoke. "Nice…"

"You can eat, but then you have to go," Galina said.

Liosha looked at her, narrowing her eyes. He had no intention of leaving, it was perfectly clear. He ate, smoked another cigarette, and went into the living room. Galina brought some beer. They sat on the couch and watched the news. Liosha put an arm around her shoulder; he had a way of trying to win her over. And what's wrong with that? Galina thought. He's lonely, too, that's why he came, for the company.

It was night, and a cool breeze blew through the open windows. Galina brought in a bowl of chips, some olives, and the leftover omelet from lunch. The plates before them were empty when the door opened and Nelly came into the room.

"Liosha, my husband," Galina said. She started to get up but Liosha pulled her back down.

"Hello," Nelly said.

"Here, come sit with us," Liosha said, making room for her on the couch.

Nelly looked at him without moving.

"What time is it? I have to give you your medicine," Galina said, realizing that she'd forgotten all about Nelly's medicine, and the drops, too.

"You're not going to give her anything," Liosha said, and gestured again for Nelly to sit.

The girl came toward them hesitantly.

"Want a beer?" Liosha asked.

"Don't, she shouldn't," Galina said.

"Yes," Nelly said, and sat down on the couch.

Liosha filled his glass and handed it to Nelly. She drank the beer down in a single gulp and licked the foam.

"Okay, enough," Galina said. But she felt numb, unable to react.

"Why won't you go outside?" Liosha asked.

"I don't want to do them the favor," Nelly said gravely.

Liosha opened another beer and sat there thinking. "Good for you," he said, and smiled. Galina elbowed him in the side, but he didn't seem to notice.

"Everyone's against me," Nelly said a little while later.

"Who's against you?" Liosha asked, speaking unusually slowly.

"The people who want me to not hold on, so I'll fall."

"To fall where?"

"Into the universe, the galaxy, I don't know." Nelly made a vague gesture. "You never know *exactly* where you might fall."

"Mmm… you've got a point," Liosha said.

Galina's face was flushed from the beer. The sound from the television was drumming into her skull. She picked up the remote to change the channel.

"Turn it off," Liosha said, "I want to think." He put his feet up on the coffee table and laced his hands behind his head. "So tell me," he turned to Nelly, "who are those people?"

"Rednose, Sparrownose, Slug and Bigear," Nelly explained. These were the various doctors who had been treating her ever since she'd left the clinic.

"I'll take care of them," Liosha said.

"They're snails in suits, a black cloud of worms," Nelly said excitedly.

"I know," Liosha agreed.

"What are you telling her?" Galina muttered.

"We'll go and find them," Liosha said. His eyes were shining. "Nelly and I are going to—"

"Wait," Galina broke in. "Wait, please…" She tried to get up but fell back down. She felt strangely dizzy. She saw Nelly watching Liosha with a blurry sheen in her eyes and then saw Liosha watching the girl, too, magnetized. With enormous effort she pushed herself up off the arm of the couch and rose to her feet. She went out of the living room and stopped in the middle of the hall. She had to do something right away, that instant. She took a few steps backward and closed the door to the living room, then stood thinking again in the middle of the hall. Quick, Galina, quick. She opened the front door of the apartment. She rang the neighbor's bell and waited. She seemed to hear footsteps somewhere inside. "Mr. Tsirimokos," she whispered. She rang the bell again. Nothing. "Can anybody hear me?" she shouted.

Breathless, she ran to the front entrance. Outside, the shops had all closed. People were coming and going on the sidewalk. She turned back. Again she seemed to hear footsteps inside Mr. Tsirimokos's apartment. She pounded on the door with her fists.

"Can anybody hear me? Can anybody hear me?"

She went back into the apartment, closed the door behind her and leaned against it. She stood there for a few minutes, breathing heavily. Then she went into the living room. "Time for us to get going," Liosha said, and held his hand out to Nelly. Nelly looked at him, then glanced at Galina and stood up.

"Wait," Galina said.

"I want to go outside," Nelly said, and started walking.

Nelly climbed down the stairs, clinging to Galina and Liosha's arms. They went out into the street. She took a few steps on her own between them.

"It's fantastic to walk without holding onto anything," she said.

"Yes," Galina said. Her heart was about to burst.

"Now I'm a tightrope walker."

"Yes, a tightrope walker," Galina repeated.

They got into the Fiat, all three of them crowding into the front. Liosha turned on the engine. The car started moving.

"A strange power has taken me under its wing," Nelly said. She hung out the window and stared, entranced.

Liosha looked at her, ecstatic, and stepped on the gas.

They sped up. The car was flying and everything else was flying, too: the kiosk, the peddlers selling grilled corn and coconut from pushcarts by the fountain, the withered foliage, the newspaper stand. The whole road was flying, disappearing into the distance. It's terrifying that not a single image stays in my head, Galina thought. Only the sky, the sparse clouds, and the moon staggering between them—only these were still.

Even worse are the tears that stick in your sockets, that won't flow. The eyes glisten but the eyelids are dry: those hard-born tears hurt the most...

"Zouzou!" the woman exclaimed.

Lea looked at the little poodle that was sniffing her shoe. Its fur was honey-colored with white splotches. "It's okay," she said.

The elevator creaked as it descended. Lea turned to look at her face in the mirror, at her eyes, lightly made up and dry. Suddenly the elevator shuddered to a stop at the ground floor. Lea hurried out and held the door open for her neighbor. The dog darted out first, wagging its tail.

Lea followed them into the street. It was cold. From a distance the square looked deserted; the pavement shone as if it had rained. A drainpipe had broken and water was pouring out onto the sidewalk. Tears, sobs, gasps, Lea thought. That was the motif that would give a rhythm to the story she was writing. But she still wasn't sure and walked quickly, hoping that if left alone her mind would find the proper form. Reaching the center of the square, she took out her cell phone to check the time. She didn't want to be late, or to arrive early. A young university student had written to her several times asking to meet her. He had seen her on TV a few months earlier and had been impressed. That was when he'd first written to her. Lea had thanked him for his kind words, but didn't respond to his suggestion of a meeting. Then the young man wrote that he had read her latest book. He was only twenty-four but the book had changed his life. I look at people differently now, he had written to her. Each of them has a story. I love people more since reading your book, he wrote. "People" was underlined. Though she hadn't found that last phrase particularly moving—in fact it had annoyed her—after putting him off several times, Lea had finally agreed to meet. I hope he's charming, at least, she thought.

She had arranged to meet him at a café close to her house. How will we recognize one another? she'd asked. I could you pick you out from a crowd of a thousand people, the young man had written. Those people again, Lea thought.

The few passersby hurried along in their heavy overcoats. A garbage truck stopped at the side of the road; two men in uniforms jumped out and started to gather cut branches and leaves from the curb. Their breath steamed in the frozen air.

The café was lit up with colored lights, like a Christmas tree. The open seating area in front was enclosed in thick plastic sheeting, and despite the cold, a few groups were sitting at low tables beside gas torches that burned with bluish flames. Lea stopped short in the entrance to the café. The young man had sent his cell phone number, it made more sense to call him than to just wander around among strangers.

"Yes?" said a neutral voice.

Lea asked if he was sitting inside or outside.

"I'm waiting here in the square," he replied.

So sure he'd recognize me he didn't dare go in, Lea thought. Then she saw a guy in a down coat coming slowly toward her. He was tall and skinny, and walked leaning to one side as if someone had unscrewed him. When he came up to her, she offered her hand, then turned hurriedly toward the café. "Shall we sit outside?" she suggested.

The young man made a vague gesture. They sat down at a table by the edge of the outdoor enclosure, next to a space heater; he settled into the chair across from her and crossed his legs.

Lea looked around for the waiter. She rose from her chair and nervously waved one hand toward the entrance of the café. On the other side of the square the two workers were loading the last of the branches onto the truck and getting ready to leave. They closed the back of the truck, got in and drove off.

"A cappuccino," Lea said as soon as the waiter came over.

"The same," said the young man. His gaze was languid and he seemed older than he was.

"So you're a student, in your last year, if I'm remembering correctly," said Lea.

"I'm still missing some credits," the young man murmured.

Out the corner of her eye Lea watched him leisurely pull a pack of cigarettes from his pocket, open it, and take out a cigarette. Then he unzipped his coat and started groping around for his lighter, staring blankly before him. He lit the cigarette, blew out some smoke, and looked around at the other customers.

The waiter set their coffees and two glasses of water down in front of them. I should have ordered a whiskey, Lea thought. She watched the young man take two packets of sugar and dump them into his cup. Why did he want to meet me? she wondered. She had met readers of hers a few times in the past; the women were always more lively, more interesting. Of course most of them, even her most avid fans, really just wanted to talk about themselves, she knew that. Like the dentist who had all her books and kept her up an entire night, taking a cue from one of her novellas, which he knew almost by heart, to tell her the story of his life in a choked-up, drunken voice. But then she'd been drunk, too, so it was fine. Now the young man was stirring the foam on his cappuccino with the little spoon. Lea thought of her story. She had started writing, with great difficulty, on her return from a trip to northern Italy; after numerous versions and ripped-up pages she had settled on a motif of despair, the music of a forbidden sorrow. Tears, sobs, gasps, she said to herself. She could've been writing right then, instead of wasting her time. She already regretted agreeing to this meeting, but it was impossible for her to get up and leave, it was too soon, it was still much too soon.

An ambulance passed by, its siren screeching. The cars jammed together on one side of the street and honked.

"So," Lea began, leaning toward the young man. "So, you like literature?" she asked.

The young man smiled.

"Do you write?" Lea persisted.

"Me?" He looked at her, surprised.

"At your age, people who like to read usually write."

"Me? No way," he said, and took a sip of his coffee.

The ambulance had stopped in front of a shoe store, blocking the road entirely.

"Unbelievable," Lea said after a while.

The young man turned to look. "What's going on?" he asked.

"The guy just walked out of that store and lay down on the stretcher so they could put him in the ambulance."

"And?" He looked at her questioningly.

"Well, he can't be that sick," Lea explained. Then, seeing his quizzical expression, she unconsciously raised her voice. "He wouldn't be walking if he was dying!" She was losing her patience. Why did this idiot want to meet me? she wondered again. She was annoyed with herself for always getting into these situations. The guy was neither interesting nor interested, not the least bit curious; he seemed completely different from the person who'd written to her so enthusiastically about her book. She noticed that one leg of his pants had ridden up, revealing a half-moon of white flesh with a few black hairs. Who knows if he's got a girlfriend, Lea thought. If someone caresses this thin, limp body.

"Do you live in this neighborhood?" he asked her.

"Yes."

"You're lucky, I'd love to live around here."

"Why don't we speak in the singular?" Lea suggested, and immediately regretted it.

"Great," the young man agreed.

He was in his last year at the university but was still missing a lot of credits. His studies didn't really interest him. He lived with his mother, who was divorced. His father had remarried. "It's no problem," he said, "we get along just fine." He had a little sister, too, from his father's second marriage, who wanted to be a flight attendant.

The young man spoke in a slow, monotonous voice. Tears, sobs, gasps, Lea thought and tried once more to find the thread of her story. One by one the words, then the sentences of the half-finished story streamed through her mind with incomparable grace, like white snowflakes swirling before they dissolve, and she realized she was fooling herself. How could she possibly believe she would get over her despair by writing about it? A month earlier everything had been different. She remembered her lover's lips, his face, his body on the unkempt bed in the room of the Italian hotel. How exquisite the timbre of his voice had been when he said her name! Lea, Lea, she said to herself, Lea, do you love me? She remembered their walks in the rain, the dark arcades of the small Renaissance city, and then a fight in a restaurant while outside thick fog descended. She remembered the anguished look in his eyes the last time they made love. That look, she should have understood right away... If she hadn't started writing, she would be crying now, crying incessantly. Yet her eyes were dry, tearless. She wished she could cry, could burst out sobbing in front of this fucking idiot.

He had met two other writers, the young man was saying. One of them had invited him to his house, he had a big cage with canaries in the kitchen. He had ordered pizza and they ate on the veranda. "Sometimes we talk on the phone. He calls me late at night when he can't sleep," the young man said and laughed.

"I've never read anything of his," Lea said. She looked furtively at the time on her phone; soon she would be able to get up and leave.

"He prints his books himself and sells them by correspondence."

"Good idea."

A sudden wind kicked up. The café awnings snapped like sails and doubled over. The flames in the heaters flickered. A few steps away she saw her neighbor with the poodle, which was running in front of her. The woman caught sight of Lea and stopped beside their table. "It's awfully cold, I hope they've turned on the heat," she said.

The poodle came closer, wagging its tail. Lea reached out a hand and the dog turned and looked at her nervously. One of its eyes was blue, the other was brown, slightly bigger and looking askew. She'd never seen a cross-eyed dog before.

"Meet Miss Zizi," Lea said, petting the dog.

"Zouzou," her neighbor corrected.

"Zou-zou," the young man repeated.

"I thought its name was Zizi," Lea said after her neighbor had left. She felt the sadness galloping through her.

"Perhaps we'll meet again in five years, or ten," her lover had said. They were standing on the station platform, hugging, her train would arrive in a few minutes and then she would leave, and the most comforting sequel, the only thing Lea could hope for, was some terrible accident, a tragedy, the train derailing as it entered the station, explosions, debris burning beside dismembered corpses. "If I ever love again it will be you," he had said, and suddenly seemed to be in a hurry to get away. I miss him so much, Lea thought, in my secret life we're still making love. She felt her eyes stinging with tears and turned to look at the torch outlined against the misty sky, its bluish flame turning silver, then yellow with black spots.

"I'd like to get a puppy, but my mom won't hear of it," the young man was saying.

Lea leaned toward him. "Dogs can suffer, did you know that?" she asked.

"You mean stray dogs?"

"No, all of them, all animals. It doesn't matter that they can't talk or think rationally or any of that. What matters is that they can suffer, a French philosopher said it. That's what should interest us, understand?"

The young man nodded. For a second he seemed to be searching for the right words but he stayed silent and kept smoking, inhaling deeply.

"I should be going," Lea said a while later. She murmured something about another appointment and got ready to leave. The young man stood up unwillingly and picked up his pack of cigarettes from the table.

"Well, it was nice to meet you," said Lea.

"But we'll meet again, right?" the young man asked. He was standing in front of her, blocking her way.

Lea looked up at him, surprised.

His face was pale and slightly sweaty.

"Yes, we'll meet again," she said and tried to smile.

The young man was still waiting.

He had drawn very close to her. His mouth was half open, like a wound, his lips cracked, with pink lines.

"Of course we'll meet again," Lea repeated. She raised a hand and touched him briefly on the shoulder, then turned and walked across the square. There was a flower stall that was still open and she headed toward it, toward the pale lights that shone on fresh tulips and scarlet roses.

wanna play?

It was a glorious summer day. A perfect morning. The soil in the flowerbeds was still cool and white steam rose into a cloudless sky. She was somewhere in the garden, riding her bicycle under tall trees with thick leaves. Around her was a frenzy of buzzing bees. A maid who occasionally performed the duties of a nanny was sitting next to the fountain, watching her little brother, though he didn't really need watching, since he just slept most of the time in a straw crib with white lace.

She must have been four years old that summer. It was around the time when she began to conceive of herself as a separate being, and one she liked. What she felt above all was a new obstinacy, a strong wave of determination, as her presence in the world became distinct. She could spend hours alone now, playing quietly in a corner or entertaining herself with a thousand different things, with a constant awareness that everything she did was confirmation of the change that had taken place, of the wonderful creature she was becoming.

"Wanna play?" the boy asked.

He was a pitiful child, a bit younger than she, barefoot, with a shaved head. He always had a string of green snot dangling from his nose. She'd been told not to go near him because he had lice. His father was their groundskeeper, a big fat man who smelled of ouzo. His family lived in a shed by the well at the edge of the property.

"Wanna play?" he asked her again with that pathetic look.

She looked him in the eye without speaking. She let her bicycle fall to the ground and started to run. She could hear his footsteps behind her. She ran around the house and up the stone steps. The kitchen door was open. She stopped to catch her breath. Everything was spotless and tidy. The pots and pans shone in the morning light, the canary was chirping in its cage. There was no one around. The house was still, as if it were sleeping. She started to run again down the hall, the boy at her heels. On her right and left were the closed doors of the bedrooms, and for a moment it seemed as if she could see right through them, to the fastened shutters, the half-dark, the beds with their white linen spreads, empty and breathing on their own in the cool silence.

She pushed open the little door next to the storage room and started up the stairs two at a time. The boy followed, panting. At the top of the stairs was a long corridor strewn with all sorts of junk. She made her way forward, leaping over old trunks, armchairs with torn cushions, broken picture frames and mirrors shrouded with sheets. She opened the last door and let the boy go inside ahead of her. The place was an enormous expanse of darkness. The air was hot and stuffy and smelled of mildew and rat poison. She waited a minute for her eyes to adjust, then closed the door.

"Ouaaaa!"

Her cry echoed like the thrust of a knife, sinking into the four walls.

Ouaaaa. That was how it always started. Shrieking, she would push the boy into the darkness and hit him as hard as she could. He would sniffle and cry out, an unbearable little yelp so feeble that no one would ever hear it or come to his rescue. She'd hit him again, again, again. She'd kick him in the stomach, pull his hair, scratch his cheeks. Then she'd give him one last push and go back out into the hall. She'd run down the stairs, then out to the garden and her toys, as if nothing had happened. She knew the boy would come back the next day and ask again if she wanted to play.

By the fountain the maid would be leaning against the straw crib, dozing. Soon her baby brother would wake up and need to eat. For a minute she would stand still, staring out at the sea. The morning light painted the cape and the few houses along the shore blue, the sea was sky-blue cream, and the only sound was the distant cawing of a gull. Then she would see her mother coming, weighed down with groceries, and would run to the front gate to help. They would go into the kitchen and put the fruit in the fridge, the sugar and coffee in their own special jars. "You're the best little girl in the world," her mother would say, kissing her.

She was the best little girl, and around that time some family friend gave her a lovely gift, a little red cap he had brought back from Iraq. The same friend had given her mother a carved silver ring with a long, narrow stone. She liked to put them both on and go out for walks in the street.

One day, as she passed by her parents' bedroom, their door was ajar and she stopped to look in. Her gaze fell on the mirror on her mother's dressing table. She looked at her own reflection and was stunned. It wasn't that she was pretty; her features were ordinary, even anonymous. It was something else. Her face was pure triumph! An all-powerful face that no one could resist. She looked at herself long and hard, trying to memorize what she saw. Then she went out into the garden to oil her bicycle.

She didn't go back to the mirror, but that image of triumph remained alive within her all summer. A feeling of omnipotence drove her at all times, when she was walking, playing hide-and-seek in the dunes, swimming off the cape.

There was one motionless moment in the garden. A heavy, metallic sky, an uneasy silence, as if a storm were gathering. It was late afternoon and the sun burned feverishly on the horizon, but under the willows and eucalyptus trees, the light suddenly flickered, then froze. For an instant all sound ceased. Invisible rattles, whispers of white noise flooded her mind. Then the leaves of the trees rustled. Insects with golden shells crawled into the bushy flowerbeds, and high above the cicadas took up their song again. As the shadows of the trees hurried over the grassy paths, she waited in silence.

Soon afternoon would become evening. Night would fall swiftly. Then she would see the boy approaching, his tiny figure slipping from light into darkness. In his whining voice he would plead, "Wanna play?"

landscape with dog

Suddenly thunder cracked. The dog rushed onto the bed and I looked at him, half asleep. In the terrible brightness that swept through the dark room, lead-colored crusts gleamed in his wide eyes as if he were blind.

Then the phone rang.

"Do you write poems?"

It was the voice of a ventriloquizing grocer, the sound that comes from a grocer's belly.

"Poems?"

"Sorry, my mistake."

And the line went dead.

I got up and walked into the kitchen. I drank some water from the fridge, staring out the window. It had started raining, a bright rain with white sideways sparks that was getting heavy. It's nice, I thought.

I opened the balcony door and the cold air hit my feet. I went back to bed. The dog was waiting for me, trembling. Aside from cats, lightning is the only thing he's scared of. I stroked him lightly while under the covers my feet pushed him gently toward the bottom of the bed.

The phone rang again.

"It wasn't a mistake," the man said.

"You must be pretty sure of yourself," I said ironically.

"First of all, forgive me for the inappropriate hour," he said, then faltered.

"You'll never believe it," I say to my friend the next morning. "Someone called last night to confess his love."

"Tell me the whole story," she says, and presses the red button.

"He's someone I met a long time ago, when I used to go to that bar where people read poems. He always sat at the same table and drank cognac."

"A poet?" my friend asks.

I'm thinking about something else just then, and as I think about it, I feel a shiver in my chest.

"What makes you say he had a grocer's voice?" she asks.

I reach out and turn off the tape recorder.

"Leave it on," she says. She wants to record everything we say. In ten years it will be a monument to our friendship.

I look at her but don't say anything.

"The nurse was the only real love of my life," I finally say.

It was a small clinic, like a villa, in the suburbs. Everyone else was anorexic and the doctor said my problem was the same, the flip side of the same coin. But it wasn't. I was bursting out of my clothes, while the others looked like skeletons. At mealtimes they would turn their heads away and stare off into space. The nurse was a former patient who volunteered at the clinic. He said his was a rare case, because there aren't many guys with anorexia.

"Don't start crying," my friend says.

I don't cry. I finish my coffee slowly. Then I hear her saying she has to go.

"I remembered a line of yours," the voice said over the phone.

I was watching the clock on the bedside table. It was exactly twenty past three. It had started raining again.

"Love, out of the arid light, you bear premature roses," the man recited, the words uprooting themselves one by one from the pit of his belly.

I waited for him to say something else but he didn't, so I lay there listening to him breathe. Outside it was still rainy and the room was cold. After a while I replaced the receiver and switched off the light.

One day I had followed the nurse. There was a gym at the clinic and beside it a pool that looked like a pond. No one ever used it. They never changed the water, and it was green, with thousands of little bugs. The nurse took off his clothes and folded them onto a plastic chair. His body was white, completely hairless, and transparent, as if steeped in moonlight. I watched him from my hiding place in the locker room. For me it was pure happiness.

The phone rang once and stopped.

I looked at the clock again. Five past four.

The dog was snoring, curled up at my feet. I fell asleep too. I dreamed that I was in a house with connecting rooms full of beds. I was pregnant. The father was the guy who kept calling, but somehow the pregnancy had occurred after the fact, or rather had been in a kind of silent hibernation since the days when I used to go to that bar and had suddenly flared up again after all these years. "I have to have an abortion," I said out loud and woke up bathed in sweat. I opened my eyes. It was still dark. Out in the street the morning traffic had begun.

Lying beside the dog, I stared at the bright patterns on the ceiling. There was one shape that looked like a helix and next to it a little white spot. The spot turned into an arrow and shot forward, the helix stayed behind while the arrow started to run from one edge of the room to the other, back and forth over the naked surface like a poem looking for the right word. Then it disappeared and the helix remained, hovering.

Outside the rain had stopped. The dog sat up on his hind legs and barked. In the half dark his eyes had a macabre look to them; it was the gaze of a dog's skull. I tried to remember the poem I'd written about the nurse. "Love, out of the arid light, you bear premature roses / Wet branches that quiver like snowdrifts," was how it continued. Somewhere a door creaked, then an invisible hand moved the curtain gently over the window. A pale aura had enveloped the objects in the room, and I waited for them to acquire outlines.

where is piazza navona?

From a distance the lights along the Tiber looked fake: streetlights wrapped in mist, lamps casting a faint, whitish glow. The rain had just stopped and the pavement shone like the belly of a fish.

"Look how high the water is," Nadine said as they drove along the Lungotevere.

She was sitting on the edge of her seat, as if she thought the roof of the car might open at any moment and she might be catapulted into the air.

Bruno threw a fleeting glance at the rising river, dark and swollen, at the black water that flooded the shores and then receded, leaving garbage and mud. He didn't say anything. He seemed absorbed in driving. His glasses reflected the lights from the street and Nadine saw an expression on his face that she had never noticed before, of exhaustion or maybe detachment.

"Where are we going?" he asked after a while.

"Didn't we decide that already? To Piazza Navona," Nadine answered.

It was the place in Rome that depressed her most, but she knew he loved it. He liked to walk at noon through the deserted piazza with the pigeons, to have an aperitif standing up and to feel inspired, narrating out loud or mentally mulling over the history of each monument, shaping a new line in his head or reworking a line he'd already written. Or did he like Piazza Navona precisely because she didn't—because it made her feel an uncontrollable impulse to run away, because he wanted to see her suffer, or even because he hoped she would leave him for good?

Nonsense, Nadine thought. They'd made love before they set out, and afterward she had lain for a while on the disheveled bed, motionless and intoxicated, listening to the rain hitting hard against the windowpanes and water splashing in the bathtub at the other end of the hall, where he was taking a shower. She remembered, with a shudder, the feeling of his body on hers. Bruno always left a certain taste on her skin, and sometimes when he was out for the afternoon or even just ten minutes, if he'd gone down to the bar for a coffee, she would search for it on her body, in her body, in different ways, casting spells, repeating motions. She would stand at the window and hold her breath until she saw him disappear behind the greengrocer's on the corner, then bite her tongue to feel the pain, and each time she would imagine she was never going to see him again, or would slowly stroke her neck to the top of her breast, stopping to press the places she believed hid her vocal cords, her larynx, her pharynx, or would put a finger deep in her cunt and then smell it and lick it, searching desperately for that exquisite, bodiless taste, until her eyes filled with tears. Then he would come home and the miracle would happen all over again.

So this is where our story begins, or rather where the end of our story begins, Nadine mused in another era, a distant future, after Bruno had disappeared from her life—or, to be precise, had walked out of her life, as he'd pointed out—and the pain of separation had begun to soften. This is where it all ends. Two lovers on their way to Piazza Navona. They get lost. That's impossible, you'll say; they're coming from the Vatican, they've gone down the Lungotevere and crossed the Ponte Vittorio Emanuele, which empties onto the Corso Vittorio Emanuele, and then you turn for Piazza Navona. Yes, but which way do you turn, right or left?

She had begun to feel anxious as they were driving across the Ponte Vittorio Emanuele. There wasn't much traffic and the few cars on the road overtook them, sliding quickly past, drivers hunched in thought over the steering wheels. In her opinion, Bruno was driving ridiculously slowly. Before her the lights of the Corso Vittorio Emanuele formed two bedraggled garlands that glowed faintly, dimming to nothing at the horizon. Which way do we turn, left or right? Nadine wondered as they left the bridge behind. The question was absurd, she made the same trip at least three times a day. But suddenly she was seized by doubt. If Campo de' Fiori is to the left, Piazza Navona must be to the right. But where is Campo de' Fiori, to the left or right? Nadine tried to imagine that she was coming from the opposite direction, from Piazza Venezia, heading toward the Tiber. In that case Piazza Farnese is to the left, she was absolutely sure of that. She could picture herself walking to the flower shop across from the French embassy. So Campo de' Fiori, which is before

Piazza Farnese if you're coming from Vittorio Emanuele, is to the left, and Piazza Navona must be to the right. But was that really how it was? She didn't feel at all sure and the more she thought about it, the more she realized she was losing all sense of direction.

"Where do we turn?" she asked Bruno.

"What do you mean?"

"To get to Piazza Navona, do we turn left or right?"

Bruno didn't answer right away. He looked at her strangely for a moment, with an expression Nadine knew well, a mixture of suspicion and tenderness.

"Where is Piazza Navona?" she asked again.

Bruno had slowed down even more. A black Alfa Romeo came up behind them, honking insistently, and Bruno swerved abruptly to the right, bringing the front of the car up onto the sidewalk. "*Vaffanculo*," he shouted at the driver of the Alfa Romeo, which pulled away with dizzying speed. Bruno opened the door and got out. The right front fender had grazed a road sign and he licked his thumb, bent over and rubbed the spot where it was scratched. He got back in the car and turned on the engine, then inched along in the right-hand lane.

"What did you say?" he asked, smiling at Nadine. He wiped his forehead with his left hand. "It's hot, don't you think?" he continued and, not waiting for an answer, turned the fan's dial to the left until the marker was in the blue zone.

Nadine stretched her legs and looked at him. She suddenly wanted to embrace him, to pull his hands from the wheel and wrap them around her, to make love right there in the car.

"Piazza Navona is to the right," Bruno said, then cleared his throat.

I want to make love with you, Nadine thought. I want you to pull my panties down to my knees and lick me slowly until I start to dissolve, until I ask you to fuck me, until I plead with you and grab you by the hair, and you keep licking me and I can't see your face.

"Let's stop by Tre Scalini first… I'd like a drink before dinner," Bruno said.

"But isn't Campo de' Fiori to the right?" Nadine asked.

Bruno looked at her with his familiar, suspicious expression.

"You're right," he said a moment later, his voice completely colorless. "Campo de' Fiori is to the right and Piazza Navona to the left."

Nadine slid even further forward on her seat and pressed her thighs together. Hold me, hold me right now, she thought. As she rummaged through her purse for her cigarettes, her hand grazed her chest. Her nipples were hard and taut. Pack in hand, she stroked her breast again. If you don't touch me, I'll start to masturbate this instant, she thought. She gripped the lighter in her hand and slowly caressed the inside of her thigh.

"Shouldn't we ask someone?" she said, and was surprised by the sound of her voice, which echoed huskily from some unknown depth.

She took a drag and blew the smoke toward the windshield. She saw an ice cream shop on the corner, colorful flags hanging from its yellow awning. An old woman was standing under the awning eating an ice cream cone, a black poodle at her side.

"Can you stop here so we can ask?" she said again.

"That's absurd," Bruno said, passing the ice cream shop. "There's nothing for us to ask. I know perfectly well where Piazza Navona is. But Nadine, I'm serious, you should really cut back on the cigarettes, your voice—"

"Left or right?" Nadine interrupted.

Her erotic mood had passed, leaving a chalky taste in her mouth.

"Right," said Bruno.

"But before you admitted it was to the left," Nadine said.

"If I said that, I was wrong," Bruno agreed. "Though actually," he went on, "now that I'm thinking about it, in the beginning I said you go right for Campo de' Fiori and left for Piazza Navona, and then I agreed with you that Piazza Navona is to the right and Campo de' Fiori to the left, in other words exactly the opposite of how you remember it."

"That's not how it was," Nadine murmured.

"What do you mean, that's not how it was? What's the point of this whole conversation?"

"That you weren't sure then and you're not sure now, so it's best if we just ask."

"Well," Bruno began, with a strained smile, "I assure you, I know exactly where Piazza Navona is."

"You don't know anything," Nadine said, and realized she was shouting. "The only difference between us is, I admit that I don't know, that I've gotten confused, while you…"

She had nothing else to say and looked stubbornly ahead.

Bruno drove the car onto the shoulder and stopped. He put on the emergency brake and hazard lights and turned to look at her.

"Go and ask if you're not sure," he said, then looked out the windshield again.

The cars behind them started to honk.

"If *I'm* not sure or if *we're* not sure?" she asked, not budging from her seat.

His composure was getting on her nerves.

"If *you're* not sure," Bruno said, stretching the word out. "I know where Piazza Navona is."

He waited a while, and then, without looking at her, started the car again.

They had gone a few blocks past the place where they should have turned either left or right and were now approaching Piazza Venezia. Nadine felt furious, trapped in her rage.

"Where are we going?" she asked.

Her eyes were burning, tears about to overflow from their corners.

Bruno stopped, looked carefully in all directions and started maneuvering, trying to turn around in the middle of the road. When he'd managed to turn, he drove a few blocks and stopped again beside the taxi stand on Largo Argentina.

"So, left or right?" Nadine asked, her hand on the door handle.

She already felt sure of a small victory.

Bruno was hunched over, fumbling with the buttons of the radio.

"Left," he answered, his voice barely audible.

Nadine got out and hurried over to two taxi drivers who were leaning against the hood of a car, talking loudly. The radio was blaring an old song, "La Zingara."

"Excuse me, can you tell me where Piazza Navona is?" she asked. She was out of breath, though she hadn't run.

"But, *bella signora...*" one of the drivers said playfully, and his friend chuckled. Then, catching sight of Bruno waiting in the car, he sobered up, rose to his full height, and pointed toward where they should go. "Piazza Venezia is behind us, you see, and Piazza di Spagna down that way, on the right..." he murmured, trying to match the tempo of the song.

"Thank you," Nadine said, about to leave, when she realized she didn't remember if the taxi driver had pointed to the left or right.

"Rome is beautiful, isn't it, *signora*?" she heard him say in a sing-song voice as she walked away.

Nadine got into the car, shut the door, and looked at Bruno. His face was pale, drained of blood. To all appearances, he had spent the whole time searching for a radio station.

"I didn't understand," she muttered. "They pointed to where it is and I forgot."

"It doesn't matter," he said, and they started off.

Months later, during a marathon of phone calls in which their relationship passed under the microscope, Bruno called Piazza Navona a turning point. He said he'd felt shaken that night, unhappy.

"When I love someone, I try to make them think I'm sure of everything, maybe because I think that's what they expect of me," Nadine heard him say on the other end of the line.

She tried to act calm, stifling the howl of the beast in her chest. Afterward, for a long time, sobbing in her bed, and later, when her tears had dried, the only thing she managed to whisper to herself was, "So he really loved me"—and that "he loved me" didn't relieve her, but weighed her down.

"Hey, read this," Bruno said, handing her an article from the newspaper.

They were sitting at a table at his favorite bar in Piazza Navona, drinking whisky and soda. Nadine was sitting at the edge of her chair with her knees pressed against the underside of his thighs, looking around absentmindedly. Tre Scalini was crowded and lively that evening. A group of young people was standing by the wooden counter, gesturing and shouting, making bets with the barman. Every so often some acquaintance would stop at their table and say hello: "Hi, Nadine, hi, Bruno... Okay, we'll talk soon..."

Nadine took the newspaper without much interest, but the headline grabbed her attention:

WATERS PRICK DOCTOR TO
SKILLED MISCHIEF

Her drink must have gone to her head. She couldn't
make any sense of it; the letters swirled before her until all
that was left was a stain of ink. She held the paper steady
with both hands and tried to concentrate.

WAITER TRICKS DOCTOR TO
KILL HIMSELF

Yesterday at 7 a.m., Antonio P., a 25-year-old
waiter, identity otherwise unknown, was
found dead in a hotel on the outskirts of
Milan. According to the investigation
conducted by the relevant division of the
Milan Police Department, the death occurred
at 10:30 the previous night. The cause of
death was identified as a mix of barbiturates,
known as a "death cocktail," that has been
used on other occasions by Doctors for a
Dignified Death, a group that supports and
illegally engages in assisted suicide. Anonymous sources say that last week Antonio P.
had repeatedly visited the group's Milan
offices at Montenapoleone 15 and had sought
help, claiming that he was suffering from
final-stage pancreatic cancer. The owner of
the Hotel Bella Madonnina, where Antonio P.
died, reported during the course of prelimi-
nary investigations that the young man had
been visited by an unidentified man at 9 p.m.

on the night of his death. The description of this visitor corresponds to an old photograph of Dr. Pino Antonuti, who heads the group Doctors for a Dignified Death. The coroner's report stated that Antonio P. had neither pancreatic cancer nor any other kind of tumor, cancerous or benign; he was, in fact, in perfect health. There is a warrant out for the arrest of Dr. Antonuti, who...

"What do you think?" Bruno asked.

He'd been leaning over her the whole time she was reading, waiting to see how she would react.

"Unbelievable," Nadine whispered. Then she lost herself again in the tepid atmosphere of the bar, clenching Bruno's calf between her knees. Behind them some customer was whining into a microphone, imitating a well-known singer. As he staggered between the tables, two girls got up, threw their arms around his waist and started singing along. Eventually the whole group by the counter joined in, their voices coming together in a tremulous cacophony. Nadine finished her drink and ordered another. Later, in a cloud of smoke and drunken voices, she tried to imagine their drive home. She remembered the dead end off Via dei Serpenti where they'd parked the car and the labyrinth of streets they'd passed through to reach Tre Scalini. Leaving Piazza Navona they had to turn right, she was sure of it.

the woman

for Markellos

The woman has many arms, like a Swiss Army knife. They sprout like branches from her body when she talks. She speaks quickly, in terse phrases, swallowing the vowels. In the morning as she drags herself from room to room putting the house in order she has only two arms, not enough for all her chores. When she cries, she has no arms at all. She hides her flushed face in her palms, fingers tugging at her aging skin—she has become a trunk shaking with sobs.

T. sits across from the crying woman, saying nothing. In all their years together he has learned that silence is the best solution.

Soon it will be dark. The woman will wipe away her tears and rise. She will leave him alone at his desk, just as she found him when she came into the room.

T. hears her moving with uncertain steps down the hall. He'd like to put on some music but doesn't dare. The woman hates music—those songs are such trash, if a person has something to say why not just say it, why screech. He looks straight ahead; through the open shutters he can see the bus stop, the little park with the stray dog, the first lights coming on in the building across the street. Then the clatter of kitchen things reaches his ears magnified, an exaggerated echo of the woman's self-sacrifice.

The woman doesn't love anyone but T., she's told him that. "I don't care if there's an earthquake and everyone else dies in the rubble, as long as you're okay. Or if there's a civil war and families wipe one another out, sons killing fathers until everyone vanishes off the face of the earth. As long as you survive."

There was a time when T. used to rehearse his suicide. Never real attempts, just rehearsals. He would lock himself in the bathroom, fill the sink with water and plunge his head under the surface. The woman would pound on the door. "Come out, what are you doing in there?" she would shout as T. opened his eyes underwater. He could picture himself, eyes bulging and rolling up until only the whites showed, bubbles escaping from his mouth, then suddenly ceasing—but it was just the image of a drowned man he'd seen on TV. "Open the door," she'd cry, "or I'll break it down." T. knew very well that the woman was capable of acting on her threat. His ears hummed; he liked to think he'd reached the point of asphyxiation.

In half an hour the woman will call him to the table to eat. Contrary to what one might expect, she isn't a bad cook. Sometimes she manages to make something quite good. The other day she made dolmades. But she has a thing about leftovers. She never throws anything away. So T. eats dolmades while she picks away at a shapeless mass of leftovers from the last ten days. Is she stingy? Not necessarily, but she's put effort into each of those dishes, each one individually and all of them together, from the beginning of her life up to today, and she doesn't want to waste any of it.

Once a year she makes galaktoboureko, always at the beginning of spring. During Carnival, to be precise. One day she looks outside and the birds are chirping, a wave of sweet-smelling air slips through the window—though this is something only she sees, there are no birds between the buildings and the air always smells exactly the same—and she turns to him and exclaims, "I'm going to make a galaktoboureko for you!" T. has never asked for anything in particular. "Don't go to so much trouble," he used to say. But by now he's learned to keep quiet—it makes no difference what he says, she's made up her mind, and whirls into the kitchen like a tornado.

So once a year the pan comes out of the oven and sits steaming on the Formica table. The creamy flesh of the galaktoboureko jiggles under its crust. No one is allowed to touch it. No one? T. is the only one here, and he's not allowed to eat it right away. First it has to cool, then the woman cuts it with an old knife. She wraps each piece separately in plastic wrap, then in aluminum foil, then puts them on a plastic plate in the refrigerator. She saves three pieces in the freezer, in case some unexpected visitor drops by. No one ever drops by.

But spring is still a long ways off; it's not even Christmas yet, and time marches inexorably forward—months don't mix, you can't just choose a season, spring today, tomorrow a heat wave, the next day rain. So T. has no idea why he's thinking about galaktoboureko as he gets up from his desk and walks slowly toward the kitchen, where the woman is waiting for him. Why has he fixated on this ridiculous detail, on the fact that while she makes the galaktoboureko specially for him, she's never once let him eat it right out of the oven? Why is he stuck on something that only seems like a paradox, when the woman herself is a walking parade of paradoxes?

T. walks into the kitchen.

"I hope you like it," the woman says. Her face is still red from crying, and she lets out a spiteful little laugh.

A chicken leg and five chunks of potato. Between him and the woman sits a bowl of salad. They start eating. If he leaves any food on his plate, even a single piece of potato, she'll complain that he doesn't give a damn about all the trouble she went to. If he cleans his plate, she'll rush to fill it again, and then he'll have another set of problems to deal with, because if he leaves a little food the second time around, she'll accuse him of waste and thoughtless gluttony, but if he eats it all, she'll serve him again, and so on and so forth.

The woman has made it clear to him, many times, that she doesn't like to cook. She hates it. She finds it disgusting, chopping up all those carcasses and smearing them with sauces. If she lived alone, she'd never cook. She'd live on honey and grasshoppers. On nothing but air. But she can't abandon him; she'd be signing his death warrant with her own hands, since he couldn't even boil a potato on his own.

"I'd like some galaktoboureko," T. says all of a sudden.

The woman looks at him. Her surprise turns into disbelief, then suspicion.

"Have you been drinking?" she asks.

"I'd like some galaktoboureko," T. says again, wondering how the idea came to him and warning himself that this may be the beginning of the end.

"Come on, open your mouth, let me smell," the woman orders.

He opens his mouth, and as the woman bends toward him, it crosses his mind that he could punch her so hard her head would crack open against the table, her brains spattering all over the tablecloth. He sits motionless in his seat and exhales into the woman's nostrils.

"Again," she says.

T. exhales again.

The woman sits back down. She wipes her face with a paper napkin, then looks at him in disappointment: she would have preferred if he'd been drinking. If he were drunk, she might have forgiven him.

"I'll make you some kourabiedes next month," she says with forced merriment.

Kourabiedes are for Christmas.

"We only make galaktoboureko during Carnival," she explains, as if talking to a retarded person.

"I'd like some galaktoboureko," T. insists.

Then the woman starts talking. It's not enough that she wears her hands down to the bone keeping the house neat and his clothes clean and ironed. It's not enough that she cooks him something different every day. As she speaks, arms sprout from her body, moving restlessly in all directions. Then she starts to sob and her body becomes nothing but trunk.

He doesn't know what's come over him. He grabs the bone from his chicken. It still has some scraps of flesh clinging to it, and all of the skin, which has grown hard. He palms the slippery bone, squeezes it between his fingers to feel the grease in his fist, and—*crack!*—throws it down on her plate.

"Eat," he says. Then he gets up from the table and walks out of the kitchen.

He could have behaved more rationally. There were other arguments he could've made: she's the one who always eats the kourabiedes, and the rest of the sweets, too; she sneaks food with the door of the fridge half open; she chews over the trash can. And the most important: she never lets him eat the galaktoboureko hot, the way he likes it.

There were lots of ways he could have handled it.

He acted like an idiot.

And now?

The woman has locked herself in her room, the upstairs neighbors are fucking, their headboard hitting the wall rhythmically, monotonously. Tock, tock. An epileptic's morse. T. looks out the window into the night. Heavy black membranes pass by, moved by some malevolent hand. If the woman believed in God, everything would be easier, he thinks. But she hates priests, in fact anything related to the church or religion. "Listen," she's warned him, "they're all crooks. When I die, don't let those bastards anywhere near me. I'd rather never find peace, I'd rather twist and turn in my grave like a zombie and kick the lid off my coffin at night and jump out." T. shudders at the thought. No, he won't call a priest.

The street between the apartment buildings is deserted. The shadow of the stray dog passes. Then a flash of lightning crosses the sky like a sigh of light. T. closes his eyes. Once the woman was pretty. T. knows that from an old album with photographs of her. The woman at the beach with two of her classmates. Who would have guessed? The woman as a baby in a little jumpsuit. He'd like to burst out laughing, lying there with his eyes closed, but he's afraid she'll hear. When he was very small, the woman used to take him into her bed. He can remember it vividly, as if it were happening now, right this minute, and he wonders how he ever could have liked it. He remembers the pink robe she used to wear, when she would pick him up and carry him to her bed and hug him so tightly he could hardly breathe. He remembers her laughter filling the room, he remembers her smell, her soft skin, her golden brown hair, he tries and tries to remember her face as he drifts off to sleep.

I've never dreamed I was running in a race, P. thought. He was driving past the Olympic Stadium and for an instant he imagined himself entering the arena, his body relaxed and his soul in his mouth, or perhaps the opposite, his heart beating calmly in its proper place and his muscles tense, showing their teeth. For a few minutes he drove absentmindedly in the lefthand lane. The stuff of his dreams had absorbed him completely. Someone behind him started to honk.

I've never worn Adidas or Nike in my sleep, P. thought, or rubbed my hands with chalk. For some reason the realization upset him. He tried to change lanes so as to turn at the next light. A Peugeot cut him off from the right, blocking his way. Why don't I ever dream about sports? he wondered as he pounded on the horn. He couldn't blame it on the fact that he was a sedentary type who had spent half his life behind a desk: he often dreamed he was flying an airplane, or even a spaceship, with no problem at all, though in his waking life he broke out in a cold sweat every time he had to parallel park. In his dreams he had tried every imaginable occupation, had traveled to distant lands, had risked his life, had died while calmly facing the most difficult situations. So why not an athlete? he wondered. Not once had he experienced the sprinter's high, the absolute ecstasy of the marathon runner nearing the finish line, still running but feeling as if he's crawling on hands and knees as he stares ahead at an imaginary point in the hazy heat, hearing the crowds cheer under the sun, his stomach tingling with the first intimations of victory, the taste of a triumph that seems almost guaranteed—and then suddenly someone overtakes him and he's losing everything at the very last minute, though it's still not entirely certain, because it's all happening in slow motion, in an astonishingly exhausting dream.

P.'s whole neighborhood was obsessed with the upcoming Olympics. The summer had begun with the slogan "Raise it high," after Greece's victory in the European Cup, and now everyone was using it in its most vulgar variation. His wife and daughter used it as an all-purpose phrase for every occasion, as did the woman at the corner store and the blind old man with the accordion who stood by the park in the evening playing mournful songs.

"Can you do a back bend?" the kids in the park asked.

The blind man smiled from behind his black glasses.

"Do a back bend for us," they insisted.

That summer P. hated kids.

And the blind man seemed to see better than a hare.

If he could have his way, he would dream himself into a swimming race. Those magical bodies, their taut shoulder blades slicing the water; those watery figures undulating like fish, touching the edge of the pool, taking a quick breath, then plunging in again like creatures from another world. That's the kind of race he'd want to dream about. Synchronized swimming was another matter altogether. Not just because it was a woman's sport, but because it seemed so ridiculous, so graceless, that he would die of shame, even in his sleep, if he were to find himself surrounded by those windup ducks with clothespins on their noses trying too hard to seem charming.

He had reached his block; now came the ordeal of parking. Just then a spot was opening up directly in front of his building, but instead of being pleased, he cursed under his breath. He would have preferred to circle the block a few times and then park somewhere at a distance, away from prying eyes. He pulled up before the empty spot and mentally repeated the steps: 1, 2, 3... He pulled forward half a meter and slowly put the car in reverse.

"Cut the wheel to the left," called the woman from the corner store, who had come out to watch. Every time he had to park, the whole neighborhood participated in the feat.

He cut the wheel to the left. The car shuddered and stalled.

"Put on the parking brake. Cut the wheel all the way. Turn the key in the ignition and ease off the brake."

I'm pathetic, he thought. The woman from the corner store had circled the car and was now leaning over the driver's-side window, peering in at him. He sat there motionless. Then, like a diver springing lightly off the board and knifing into the water, a brilliant idea sliced into his mind.

"I just have to run up and get something from the apartment, I'm leaving again right away," he said.

He opened the door, politely pushed the woman aside and ran into the building.

He smiled at himself in the elevator mirror. A champion of little lies, he thought with satisfaction.

His wife and daughter were watching TV in the living room with the air conditioner on.

"There's pizza," his wife called from behind the closed door.

It was the summer of pizza.

From the living room he could hear music, then voices, then a jumble of shouts and something like horses' hooves pounding on pavement.

"Raise the fucker high!" the two women shouted in unison.

P. went out onto the balcony and looked down.

The woman from the corner store was still standing next to the stopped car, which was blocking half the road.

"Dad," his daughter called, then more loudly, "What are you doing, Dad?"

P. went back into the apartment and stood by the front door.

"I have to go back to the office," he said.

"There's pizza in the oven," his wife said.

"Come here, Dad, I want to tell you something,"

"I won't be late."

Through the glass in the living room door he could make out their silhouettes, dark and fluid like wings on a distant horizon.

"I have work to do," he said, more to himself than to anyone else.

Instead of leaving he went back out onto the balcony.

The woman had gone back into her store. The road was dark now, sunk in lethargy. Only his car with its white roof and its snout blocking the road seemed ready to spring into action.

He looked at the building opposite. It was still covered in netting. During the day men worked, unseen, on the scaffolding under the nets. Now it was completely silent. During the day you could hear hammers, pickaxes, pneumatic drills. P. often listened to the workers arguing in foreign languages. Sometimes they would whistle at a girl walking by. He never saw them. There were others who worked at night, burrowing into the roads. Digging ditches and laying cables. Every morning the sidewalks were torn up and there were thick clouds of dust in the air. He wondered what would happen when the construction was finished. Where all those people would go, if the ditches would swallow them up.

Leo and I
facing each other
I talk about my love.

Leo is a dog, eleven years old. Sometimes I hide his age for no reason. I might mumble vaguely that he's "about four," or stare absentmindedly at something over his shoulder while saying that he's "just two and half, a puppy, really." The fact that he's still quite mischievous and stubborn makes things easier.

On summer nights when friends gather on the veranda, Leo goes wild. I know it's because he wants to be loved, wants to win over each guest individually, but most people get frightened or annoyed. Anyhow, he calms down after an hour or so. If he finds an empty chair he'll jump up and sit in it. He doesn't curl up, doesn't sleep. Stiff, formal, his back against the back of the chair and his eyes wide open, he follows the conversation, turning his head to look at whoever's speaking. He's a solemn, sensitive listener, perfectly aware of how charismatic he is.

Leo and I
facing each other
I talk about my love.

The day falls
through a trapdoor
of cherry dust.

We both have the same sign. We're Gemini, born thirty-nine years apart. Sometimes on winter nights I dream that I have no head. I never used to get headaches. Now I'm an insomniac, too. Twisting and turning in bed, I'm plagued by the most dreadful thoughts; the screen of my mind shows a puzzle of decomposing shades: light gray, smoke gray, thick black, and finally white. White? Yes, white is the color of my very worst premonitions. I get up, turn on the light and drink some water. I go into the living room. Leo wakes up and follows me. We sit in two armchairs. We look at each other silently. Sometimes I talk to him.

Leo and I
facing each other
I talk about my love.

The day falls
through a trapdoor
of cherry dust.

Evening already
Leo and I
in our armchairs.

Can a failed poem haunt someone for three months? Can it give shape to an entire fall, and even after that, when the first cold snap comes, can the line "I tell him of my love" still prowl through my head at the most unlikely times, as I'm waiting at a crowded bar, parched for whiskey, or standing with one foot in the tub, shivering, unable to decide whether or not to get in?

It's Christmas, and Leo and I are watching the lights on the tree. Time passes. It's quiet outside. I get up and go to my desk. I read the same poem again, make a few changes. Leo looks at me, disappointed. He hates anything to do with writing.

"Don't look at me like that, you're ruining my inspiration," I say. "Just give me ten minutes."

Leo starts to fidget.

"Calm down, Leo," I say. "I'll tell you a story."

Leo barks.

I abandon the poem, go back and sit next to him on the sofa.

"In Sicily there was this restaurant, La Luna, on a cliff near Syracuse. The sea shone in the moonlight and in the distance fishing boats were pulling up their nets. Our table was on the edge of the cliff with the sea stretched out below, and you could hear the roar of waves breaking against the rocks. The waiter told us that in the old days the place had been a Saracen fortress.

"The man was very attractive. But ugly, too. He had a long nose with craters, like a little outcropping of land left after Etna erupted. He bought me camellias. We held hands over the tablecloth. He squeezed my hands in his, which were warm and dry, then bent and kissed them. His belt must have been too tight because when he straightened up again he was bright red and out of breath. What was I wearing? A short skirt and a black shirt that said 'Crocodiles are fun.' I didn't love him, but I was drawn to him. He was unbelievably clean, because he sweated a lot and was always showering.

"When we got back to the hotel he told me to wait, then shut himself in the bathroom for a long time. I didn't know what to do, so I turned on the television with the sound off. There had been a terrorist attack in Palermo, the mafia had ambushed the car of some important judge. I'll never forget the screams of the carabiniere's wife before the camera as she crouched over the wreck that contained her husband's mutilated body. It was harrowing and very beautiful, with an uncanny plasticity. Her mouth opened and closed, but no sound came out. She looked like a girl, no more than sixteen or seventeen, but she was the wife of the carabiniere who had been head of the garrison.

"Anyway, the man showed no sign of emerging from the bathroom. Every so often the toilet flushed, the water in the shower would come on, then there would be a few seconds of absolute silence before the toilet flushed again. I opened the mini fridge, took out a chocolate bar with raisins and lay down on the bed, fully dressed.

"'Do you need the bathroom?' He was standing in the door, leaning toward me, smiling uneasily. He was wearing a white bathrobe with the hotel monogram, and water was dripping from his hair.

"I shook my head, returning his smile. He closed the

bathroom door gently behind him and a while later I heard the hum of the hair dryer. On the television they were interviewing the chief of police and former classmates of the carabiniere. I turned the volume up a little. 'It's an outrage, a colossal outrage,' said a trembling old man in a brown cap and striped shirt. 'It's the government's fault, the real murderers are in Rome, in Parliament, feeding themselves with silver spoons…' He was standing in front of a watermelon stall. A woman came into the frame, grabbed his arm and pulled him out of sight. Now the camera was moving shakily down a country road. The image was clear, but the frame kept shifting. We were going to the carabiniere's village, to his parents' house. A tiny settlement appeared, clinging like a wasps' nest to the rocky hillside. The road into the village and the first few houses had been destroyed by landslides. We arrived at the central square and stopped in front of a church of astonishing beauty. The façade was pink and weathered. The bells rang sadly. Then the camera turned 180 degrees and showed three old men sitting outside a coffee house. They frowned at us, then looked away.

"I turned down the volume when I saw him coming in. He lay down next to me on the bed, propping himself up on his elbows. He was still wearing the bathrobe and smelled of cologne, with bergamot and something else, dry and heavy, maybe ash.

"'Let's get undressed,' he suggested, without looking at me. He set his glasses on the nightstand, took the remote control, turned off the television and dimmed the light.

"I took off my skirt and the shirt that said 'Crocodiles are fun.'

"He kept his robe on.

"'I'm embarrassed to take it off because I'm fat,' he said.

"That was it! I felt a storm of tenderness and fell for him right away. To this day, I still don't know how it happened. The only explanation is that a man who acknowledges a weakness, a flaw, immediately acquires tremendous sex appeal.

"Shortly before dawn, he got up and opened the window. The curtains quivered and from a distance we could hear dogs howling and running. He turned over in the bed and embraced me. A few minutes later the room had filled with the scent of jasmine. Were there flowers outside the window? I never found out.

"'Since the tide is rising and rising, shall the two of us swim?' I asked.

"'Say that again,' he mumbled, half asleep.

"'Since death and its time will come, shall the two of us die?' I asked.

"It was a song from some tribe in Africa, I don't know what made me think of it just then. He smiled faintly in the half light as if he hadn't heard."

I look at Leo, who's listening, absorbed.

"That's life, just so you know," I say, finishing the story. "That's how I stepped in it and fell in love."

Leo looks at me, uneasy. He's waiting for the rest of the story. Outside the fireworks have started.

"There's nothing else," I explain, trying to sound cheerful. "It all ends here."

We listen to the fireworks in silence. Muted flashes tear through the room, unreal lighting that transfixes me.

Then Leo starts to bark.

"I never saw him again, that was that," I insist.

He isn't satisfied with the denouement. He wants something more, I know. A happy ending or some big drama. But there's nothing I can do. That something doesn't exist. And I don't want to lie to him. For a while we eye one another, tense as a dog and cat. Then he lays his head on my shoulder and sighs deeply. We sit there side by side, motionless, watching the lights on the tree.

rain at the construction site

At two in the afternoon when the men went back to work Loukas always took a break. He would grab a beer, stand on the step outside the canteen and light a cigarette, staring out at the curve in the road where the freshly laid pavement twined gently around the foothills of the mountain and disappeared into the mouth of the tunnel. He had never made it that far, but he knew that just past the curve the road stopped abruptly, dangling like a severed arm over the swollen river. A few hundred meters further down was the old road, with its potholes and sagging guardrails. The trucks had to drive over it several times a day, bringing materials to the site.

Loukas had been following the progress of the work closely these past few months. He had begun to take it personally. It seemed to him that the construction wasn't moving fast enough, wasn't going at the pace he would have liked. "What do you care?" the men would bark at him, annoyed. Sooner or later the road would get built, that was their philosophy. "Are you in such a rush to be out of work?" the foreman would joke.

It had been a warm spring day, but then the weather changed and it started to rain. Loukas went inside and quickly shut the windows and door so the canteen wouldn't flood. Within a few minutes the rain had grown stronger and was lashing the corrugated metal. The hinges creaked and the prefab shook on its base as if the earth were quaking. The rain let up a little. Loukas waited, standing in front of the open tubs of butter and cheese. He tightened the valve under the sink and hesitated, listening to the water's mournful gurgling.

In his youth he had known better times. For years he had worked as a waiter on the ferry line from Patras to Ancona and had made a good living. He got married and they had a beautiful little girl with velvety eyes and skin like sugar. One summer the captain let him take his wife and daughter on a free trip. Something happened on that trip that still wasn't clear in his mind. His wife and daughter disembarked in Ancona to go shopping and never came back. Three months later he got a letter postmarked La Spezia, asking for a divorce. That was ten years ago and he hadn't seen either of them since.

There was still an hour and a half before the shift would be over and Loukas was wondering if it was worth it to wait. The flashes of lightning on the horizon had become denser and a screen of mist hid the construction site, the machinery, the crane. The curve of road at the base of the mountain was completely invisible. Then the rain stopped as suddenly as it had begun. Everything around him was mud. He gathered his things and locked the canteen. He put the key in his pocket and started walking gingerly, careful about where he put each foot.

A few weeks earlier his daughter had called. She was sixteen years old and in high school. He was dying to know how she'd gotten his number and whether she'd called entirely of her own accord, but he didn't ask. He learned that his wife had remarried, a man named Claudio who had a butcher shop, and that they all lived together in La Spezia. He didn't dare ask if Claudio had been the one to take them from Ancona. The lines of communication were still fragile; he didn't want to put pressure on the situation. One wrong move and it would be over. But if he was careful, he might convince his daughter to see him; he could go to Italy, or she could come to visit him that summer. Since then they had talked twice more.

"I'll tell you a story," he'd said during their last conversation. "When you were little, you were always getting the hiccups. Your mother and I were very young and didn't know anything about babies, so we worried. We would pick you up and walk with you through the house until the hiccups stopped. Once your mother started crying because she was scared you might stop breathing and I took you down to the harbor. I showed you the seagulls, the boats, and told you all about them…"

"Then what happened?" his daughter broke in impatiently.

"The hiccups stopped."

"That's the story?"

"Yes," Loukas replied, with the vague impression that his daughter had been expecting something else.

A Ford Fiesta was stopped at the edge of the old road, its hood open. A woman in a red coat and black heels was bent over, examining the engine.

"I was trying to exit onto the Egnatia highway, but something happened to the car," she said when she saw him approaching.

"The Egnatia isn't ready yet."

The woman eyed him suspiciously. She looked about thirty-five, perhaps a bit older. She'd had her hair done but it had gotten wet and little tufts were curling up on her forehead.

"That part of the road isn't finished," Loukas explained.

"I thought…" the woman began. "I'm in a real hurry," she added with a sideways glance.

Loukas leaned over to look. He didn't know much about engines, and his first impression was of a gaping abdomen with the guts all mixed up; the battery seemed to be in the wrong place and he noticed a little spiral-shaped wire sticking out.

"Is there a flashlight?" he asked.

The woman shook her head.

The end of the wire was glowing and Loukas fumbled around blindly trying to figure out where the other end led. The wire came loose without his even pulling it and lay there in his hand like a tiny snake.

"It doesn't matter," the woman said, though from the expression on her face it was clear she was on the verge of collapse. "I'm in a real hurry," she muttered again.

Fat raindrops started to fall, and another streak of lightning tore through the sky on the far side of the mountain.

"What if we were to smoke a cigarette?" the woman suggested.

Loukas wasn't sure if she wanted his company or was just feeling hopeless. They got into the car and pulled the doors shut.

"I have an appointment and I'm very late," she said. She bit the filter of her cigarette and sighed.

Loukas took his cell phone from his pocket.

"The thing is, I can't call," the woman said. Then she was silent, watching the rain fall against the windshield.

He hadn't found out much about his daughter's life in Italy. Mostly she asked the questions and Loukas answered. Sometimes her questions were so specific that he suspected they had come from her mother. His daughter wanted details about his life and work, how he spent his days, and above all who he saw.

"Yesterday a Chinese guy came by."

"You're kidding."

"No, it's true."

"Did he buy a sandwich?"

"Of course."

"And to drink?"

"A coke and a bottle of water. But I lost lots of customers because of him," Loukas said, and explained that as soon as the Chinese guy showed up, all the workmen disappeared because they were afraid of some kind of pneumonia that had just broken out in Asia. The Chinese guy didn't pay any attention, just ate a double egg and sausage sandwich. He spoke broken Greek and said he was a reflexologist from Bangkok.

"Bangkok is in Thailand."

"Then he was Thai," Loukas said and laughed nervously.

"What happened next?"

Loukas had exhausted that episode. "A nun came once," he said, hoping to continue the conversation.

"I don't believe you."

"Yes, she was a young nun and had studied literature."

"What was she doing in the middle of nowhere?"

"I don't know," Loukas said. The nun had parked her car, an old station wagon, in precisely the spot where he was now sitting with the woman, and had walked over to the canteen, her habit blowing in the wind. She was very young and cheerful but he'd been in a bad mood that day and didn't feel like talking.

"Well, bye," he heard his daughter say.

"Wait a second," Loukas said, and immediately regretted the pleading tone in his voice.

"I have to hang up," the girl said.

That had been ten days ago, and she hadn't called again since.

The woman took off her red coat and folded it carefully over her knees. Then she moved it to the back seat. "Now what do we do?" she asked.

"We could call a tow truck," Loukas suggested.

"It's too late," the woman said, drumming her fingers on the steering wheel, "there's no point."

"I could go over to the site and see if anyone there knows about engines."

"Are you deaf?" the woman snapped. "There's no point, no one will be waiting for me now." Her eyes had welled with tears. She turned toward him. "I'm sorry," she said. With her right hand she squeezed his arm. "I'm sorry," she said again.

There were lots of things he didn't tell his daughter, things he would never tell her. Like the fact that the Chinese guy, or Thai, had turned out to be a con man and drug dealer: they'd arrested him two days later and found two bags of pure heroin in the thin mattress he supposedly used for his reflexology. Or that the nun had been very pretty but also lame, with one leg shorter than the other and twisted like a rabbit's, and the workmen had made dirty comments behind her back.

Outside, the rain was coming down as hard as ever. Perhaps he should go. There was no reason for him to be sitting in this strange woman's car if he couldn't help her.

The woman opened her purse, pulled out a flask, and drank from it. "Whiskey," she said, offering it to him.

"Thanks," Loukas said and took a long swig.

"Maybe it's better this way," the woman said, shaking her head.

"Are you married?" she asked after a while.

"I was."

"I still am," she said and shook the flask to see if there was any whiskey left. "And it looks like it's going to stay that way!" she added in a sour tone.

Loukas didn't reply. He took the flask from her and drank, staring straight ahead. The windows had fogged up from their breath, or maybe the alcohol had blurred his vision. He gave the flask back to the woman and wiped the windshield with the back of his hand. The woman pressed a button and the wipers started moving. The construction site and the crane appeared, topped by a halo of mist. The road slipped and disappeared into the mouth of the tunnel and the image looked to him like a postcard of scenery blanketed in snow.

He'd always had a weak character, that was why his wife left him. There were so many things he would never tell his daughter, things he would never dare say. He wouldn't tell her that he lived in a dump and slept on a mattress on the floor or that his landlady was an old hag. He wouldn't tell her that he had no money, or that when the road was finished he'd have nowhere to go. Or that sometimes he drank so much he passed out and when he woke up in the morning he couldn't remember anything. Or that he had no friends, or that the few women he'd been with since her mother left had been whores.

"When will the work be done?" the woman asked.

"They plan on three more months," Loukas said, "but it might be sooner."

"Great work," she said and laughed ironically. One of her eyes wandered to the right and when she laughed her face had a funny, childish expression.

"My name is Iota," she said after a while.

"Loukas," said Loukas.

"Did you know that the Egnatia is an extension of the Via Appia?" his daughter had asked.

He hadn't known. "Meaning?"

"You mean you work right next to the Egnatia and you have no idea?"

He had to admit he had no idea.

"When the Romans started building it, they had a plan in mind. They wanted to unite Italy with Greece, the West with the East, that was the goal. We learned about it in school. But of course there was always the sea in between…"

There's always the sea in between, Loukas repeated in his head. For an instant his daughter's words assumed astronomical dimensions and made him feel a kind of vertigo, an emptiness in his stomach.

"Hold me," the woman said, and Loukas obeyed. With his free hand he felt in his pocket for the key to the canteen. If the woman decided to stay with him, they could sleep there, cramped as it was. In the room he rented the landlady didn't permit guests.

Though nothing had happened, the woman started to cry in little dull sobs. Her shoulders shook and she hunched up like a puppy as he drew her to him. She was warm and unbelievably soft in his arms and her hair smelled of iodine or sulphur, something pungent and sharp.

"I'm sorry," the woman whispered, starting to pull away. "It's nothing, it just comes over me every once in a while."

"It's okay," Loukas said. "Cry if it does you good."

He held her tighter and felt calm.

He didn't want to think ahead, make any plans for the future. He didn't want to wish for something that wouldn't happen. The road would move forward on its own behind the mountain, out of his sight, and one day the severed arm would emerge from the tunnel whole.

acknowledgments

I would like to thank the House of Literature in Paros, the Instituto Sacatar in Itaparica, and the Baltic Center for Writers & Translators for the gift of a great place to work. I feel immensely grateful to Evelyn Toynton, attentive and sensitive reader, whose help has been precious at each stage of this adventure. Many thanks to Karen Emmerich for her remarkable work and her patience with my obsessions over the past two years. Thanks also to Toula Kontou, the untamed dentist, for her advice on several occasions. And much gratitude to Hilary Plum, whose passionate concern for every detail and finely tuned ear for language have made her the ideal editor. I am fortunate to have worked with her.

—*Ersi Sotiropoulos*

There are many who deserve thanks for their help in translating the stories in *Landscape with Dog*. First of all Ersi herself, for her close collaboration, and Hilary Plum, for her unfailing energy and keen editorial eye. Pam Thompson was a wonderful reader for the stories, as were David, Helen, and Michael Emmerich. I would also like to thank Peter Constantine, Constanze Guthenke, and Katerina Stergiopoulou for reading selected stories and offering advice at a crucial point in the process.

—*Karen Emmerich*